Scobie suspected nothing . . .

Up in the loft Ike Skerrit's revolver lined at Scobie. Then a sudden shock ran through the killer as he realized that the dogs gave warning of his presence.

Shooting out of his left hand, Scobie thrust the girl aside. In the same move he began to drop to his right knee and his other hand reached for the Colt Lightning rifle. Whipping the rifle to his shoulder, Scobie lined it up to where Skerrit showed blacker than the dark outline of the loft's door and squeezed the trigger. The rifle crashed loud in the night.

Something splashed wetly on to the floor behind the ladder. Scobie looked down. It was the killer's blood.

J. T. EDSON'S FLOATING OUTFIT WESTERN ADVENTURES

J. T. EDSON'S
CIVIL WAR SERIES

OTHER BOOKS BY J. T. EDSON

J.T. Edson

HOUND DOG MAN

CHARTER BOOKS, NEW YORK

This Charter book contains the complete
text of the original edition.
It has been completely reset in a typeface
designed for easy reading and was printed
from new film.

HOUND DOG MAN

A Charter Book/published by arrangement with
Transworld Publishers, Ltd.

PRINTING HISTORY
Brown Watson edition published 1967
Corgi edition published 1969
Charter edition/June 1989

ISBN: 1-55773-206-X

Charter Books are published by The Berkley Publishing Group,
200 Madison Avenue, New York, N.Y. 10016.
The name "CHARTER" and the "C" logo are trademarks belonging
to Charter Communications, Inc.

PRINTED IN THE UNITED STATES OF AMERICA

10 9 8 7 6 5 4 3 2 1

*For "Doc" Sherman, George Hallam,
Eddie Hardman, "Fingers" Lomas,
Jim Anstey and all other Army dog
men.*

CHAPTER ONE

No Chore for an Amateur

With the spring sun warming its bones, the big Absaroka grizzly bear felt a need for more substantial food than the grasses, sedges, roots and sprouting buds which had been all its stomach could take on emerging from its semi-hibernation. All through the frost, snow and storms of the winter, the bear slept secure in a snug hole beneath a deadfall of logs high in the Eastern Wyoming mountains. Hungry wolves found the den-hole, but did no more than pause, sniff around it and then lope on bristling their fear and hate of the animal inside. Even *carcajou*, the wolverine, fearless hunter and killer though it could be, ignored what might appear to offer an easy meal. Despite its other name, glutton, the wolverine knew better than enter the den of a sleeping male grizzly bear; undisputed master of the Wyoming high country.

Standing with one forefoot on a fallen, rotten log, the bear looked out over the rolling forest-covered slopes of its kingdom. With a body length of some eight foot and shoulder height of a good forty-eight inches, the bear had seven hundred and fifty pounds of well-equipped power to enforce its desires. Belonging to the Big-Toothed sub-species of *Ursus Horribilis,* its well-muscled jaws carried long canine teeth and powerful crushing molars designed for a

1

carnivorous diet. Long yellowish-brown hair hid the winter-gaunt state of its body and gave it an appearance of even greater bulk. Steel-hard, sharp and long claws projected from its feet pads, weapons of murderous efficiency which exceeded its powerful mouth. All in all, the grizzly gave the impression of being what it was, the most dangerous animal on the American continent.

A powerful blow from one paw burst open the log as if a charge of dynamite exploded inside it. Grubs and insects exposed by the blow wriggled frantically in an effort at escaping from the hated daylight. Lowering its head, the bear licked up the insect life with its tongue. Such minute morsels could not even start to appease the gnawing hunger.

Instinct, or maybe memory of other years, started the bear walking downhill. All the time as it moved, it foraged for food. Rolling over rocks, exploring bushes, it took anything which came its way, yet the hunger persisted. Rich and tempting to the bear's nostrils came the scent of mule deer. However, long experience had taught the grizzly that only a sick or injured deer was likely to fall victim. So the bear wasted no time, but continued head downwards.

Out on the more open rolling land could be found a much easier prey, one a comparatively slow-moving bear might stalk and kill. While the bear could gallop at around thirty miles an hour, raising it to thirty-five during the short burst of a charge, mule deer, elk, or the pronghorn antelope of the open range were all capable of higher speeds. Not so the animal which the hungry bear sought.

On walked the grizzly in that seemingly slow, careless, but mile-eating way of its kind. Finding one of the trails it used upon other such forays into the low country, the bear ambled along it. At intervals along the trail it found a "bear" tree. Halting, the grizzly reared up on its hind legs against the trunk and sniffed over the surface. No other bear had used the tree, as its nose showed, so the grizzly proceeded to mark a warning to others of its kind. Sinking its teeth into the bark as high as it could reach, the grizzly ripped out several chunks and dropped them on to the growing pile left by previous years' markings. With proof of occupancy made, the bear continued its quest for food.

Towards noon, as it moved through budding blueberry bushes, the bear picked up the scent it sought. With surprising silence and stealth, considering its bulk, strength and clumsy build, the bear wended its way through the bushes, following the wind-born aroma. Approaching the edge of the bushes, the grizzly slowed down and crept forward inch by inch until it could see through to the open land beyond. There, not ten yards away, the animals it came down from the high country to seek stood grazing with a complete lack of caution.

In many ways the white-faced Hereford cattle proved superior to the Texas longhorn stock they fast replaced in the mid-1890's. They produced a better class of beef and more of it per animal, were more tractable, safer to handle, bred as well without supervision and generally showed a far higher profit margin. Yet in one major respect the whiteface could not even begin to compare with its predecessor. The longhorn had been at best only semi-domesticated, possessing all the wary alertness of a wild creature and a damned good defensive armament in the six to eight foot spread of sharp horns.

Grazing contentedly and in a heedless manner no longhorn ever adopted, the small bunch of Rocking D Herefords just asked for the trouble soon to come. One of the cows moved away from her companions, drawing ever closer to the blueberry bushes and the bear's ambush position. Measuring the distance with its eyes, the bear held down an inclination to rush out. Age brought wisdom that refused to allow hunger pangs to cause a premature charge.

At last the moment came. With a coughing roar, the grizzly burst from the bushes as if they did not exist. Even then a longhorn might have escaped, or made a fight, but the white-face lacked the speed for one and instinct for the other. Paralysed by fear for a vital instant, the cow failed to react to the danger. Rearing up, the grizzly struck out with the paw that burst open the log. Bones snapped as the paw caught alongside the cow's head and broke her neck. Even as her companions scattered in belated fright, the stricken cow collapsed to the ground.

Normally the bear would have dragged its kill into the forest before feeding, covering it with debris when full and lying up close by to protect it from marauders. With winter-hunger tearing at its belly, the grizzly could not spare the time. Licking the blood which dripped from gashes torn by its claws, the bear put the final touch to its appetite. The powerful jaws closed on flesh and tore out a sizeable chunk. As the meat slid down its throat, the grizzly felt a warm satisfaction welling inside it. That first bite meant winter had gone and days of good feeding lay ahead. Overhead the first of the turkey vultures made its appearance, circling high in the sky and knowing better than drop while the grizzly fed.

Old Wilkie Wilkinson saw the circling vultures—for others soon gathered when the first located a possible meal —as he rode across the Rocking D's range on his way to the town of Desborough. Being conscientious, he put aside thoughts of recreation until after investigating the cause of the birds' gathering. After covering about a mile, he halted his horse on a rim and studied the cow's body as it lay close to the blueberry bushes.

Even from where he sat, Wilkie could tell that a bear killed the cow. Not a black bear either, but a grizzly, or that broken neck lied. Although he could see no signs of the bear, Wilkie remained at a distance. A man did not ride the

Western ranges for some thirty-five or more years without learning a few lessons, including the value of caution. He knew a damned sight better than approach a grizzly bear's kill, even in the bear's absence, when armed with only a Colt Peacemaker and Winchester Model 1866 carbine. Being of a conservative nature, he had never seen the need to waste money on the purchase of a more modern, powerful, centre-fire rifle; although he admitted, if only to himself, that the old rim-fire "yellow boy" had its limitations. Twenty-eight grains of black powder did not, to his mind, constitute adequate power when a man stood likely to tangle with a grizzly bear.

If Wilkie knew anything about grizzly bears, and he figured he did, the cow's killer ought to be in the bushes sleeping, unless it was down on Trout Creek taking a drink. In either case, being jealous of its kill, it would charge out and attack any living creature which approached the cow. Not wishing to force the issue, Wilkie turned his horse and urged it at a better pace towards Desborough. Once a grizzly started killing stock, it formed the habit and must be stopped. Wilkie figured he knew the best way to accomplish the stopping.

An hour after finding the cow, Wilkie rode towards the John Barleycorn saloon on Desborough's main—and only —street. The usual bunch of town loafers sat on the porch and all studied the old cowhand's lathered horse with interest.

"Is Daniels inside?" he asked.

"Went on over to Reiger's place to test a batch of applejack," big, bulky and well-dressed Copson, the local butcher, replied. "You look like you've been pushing your horse some, Wilkie."

"Some," admitted Wilkie.

"You got trouble?" Copson inquired hopefully.

"Depends on what you call trouble," countered the cowhand.

"What kind do you have?"

"A grizzly done took one of our cows out by Trout Creek."

"Where's its hide?" asked the butcher. "I'll buy it off you."

"The boss owns the cow's hide," Wilkie answered. "And last trail count the bear was still wearing his."

Something about the burly butcher always put a burr under Wilkie's saddle. The old cowhand never cared for Copson's attitude of breezy friendliness, which always put him in mind of a city politician hand-shaking for votes come election-time. So he prepared to ride on in search of his boss at Reiger's general store.

"You mean you didn't get the bear?" demanded Copson, grinning at his cronies, then glancing back at Wilkie.

"Well now, I sort of figured the bear might give me an argument about being got."

A guffaw broke from Copson's lips. "So now you're here looking for your boss to help out?"

"That's about the size of it," admitted Wilkie. "I figure he'll call in Scobie Dale."

"The hound dog man," grunted Copson. "Why bother with him? Reese here's got a real good hound."

"Ain't gainsaying his Lou bitch's good—for running coon, or treeing a squirrel," replied Wilkie.

"She'll trail anything I lay her to," put in Reese, indignantly defending his newly purchased dog.

"Never yet saw a red-bone's'd go again' a black bear— and that out there's a grizzly 'less I miss my guess."

"So?" snorted Copson.

"Mister, a grizzly starts being mean where a black bear leaves off," Wilkie explained patiently. "And the red-bone's never been whelped that'll tangle with either of 'em.''

"Then we'll take my Vic dog along," the butcher stated. "He'll fight anything that lives and breathes."

"Hunting a grizzly's no chore for amateurs," Wilkie insisted, making the word come out as "hammer-chewers." "I'll go tell the boss."

With that Wilkie started his horse moving and rode on in the direction of the general store. Copson watched the old man go and let out a barking snort of annoyance. Never a man to be put off once he made up his mind, the butcher determined to hunt the bear.

"Let's get the dogs," he said, turning to his cronies.

None of the loafers, especially Reese, showed any enthusiasm at the idea. While living in the Wyoming range country, they were town-dwellers who rarely went beyond Desborough's limits. Reese bought the red-bone, having her shipped in from the East, because he wished to enter the society of a group of prominent citizens whose prime interests in life centred on hunting and fishing. By owning a trained coon hound, he hoped to join the select group and gain numerous financial benefits from his acceptance. So he did not relish the idea of putting the dog on to a grizzly bear's trail.

"I can't rightly go just now, Cop," Reese finally said.

"Then we'll borrow that Lou bitch and go without you," replied Copson, not easily put off. "Won't we, boys?"

Suddenly all his companions started to remember other, more pressing business which prevented them from leaving town. Their refusal only served to strengthen the butcher's intentions.

"All right," he snapped. "I'll go by myself—if you'll loan me the bitch, Reese."

For a moment Reese hesitated, then saw the tightening of the butcher's lips and a warning glint coming to Copson's eyes. Reese owed the butcher a fair sum of money, a loan the other kept like the sword of Damocles over his head, and was altogether in no position to refuse the request. Reluctantly he nodded his agreement and went along with Copson to hand over the dog.

At the store Wilkie learned that his boss had gone along to a nearby stream to watch the local doctor try out a new trout-fly just arrived from the East, so followed Daniels to pass on his disturbing news.

After collecting the red-bone bitch, Copson went to his home and made ready for the trip. He saddled his horse, slid his Winchester Model 1876 carbine into the saddleboot and turned loose his own dog.

In a way, Copson's dog Vic was just as much a status-symbol—although the term had not yet come into use—as the red-bone hound. Copson did much business in the State capital, Cheyenne, and his eye was on a seat in the Legislature. To improve his chances, he cultivated a sporting set of business and political men in the capital. The sports went in for such diversions—from a spectator angle—as boxing and wrestling, while indulging in cock and dog-fights for added entertainment. To win membership into the select association, Copson kept a fighting dog of some ability. He figured the dog to be a match for anything that breathed and aimed to prove his point.

At thirty-eight pounds, Vic could have modelled for the ideal type of bull-terrier bred in the Cradley Heath area of England for the purpose of fighting with others of its kind. Instead of being the somewhat leggy breed favoured in the Walsall country, or the lighter, more terrier-like dog of the Darlaston district, Vic showed a bulldoggish appearance. With a short, deep, broad skull, its pronounced cheek muscles, short fore-face and level mouth telling of enormous, crushing power of bite, short, muscular neck, tremendous spring of ribs and depth of chest, the dog gave an immediate impression of controlled, deadly toughness. Vic walked in a mincing, springy manner, sharply tapered tail drooping like a pump handle, looking ready for anything.

Only Copson's presence and unceasing watch prevented Vic from attacking the bitch, for a Staffordshire bull-terrier trained for the fighting-pit lived only to try conclusions with other dogs. In fact Copson finally solved his problem by hoisting Vic on to the horse's saddle and keeping the dog there while the bitch trotted along at his side.

Spiralling turkey vultures guided Copson to the kill, as the first arrival had done with Wilkie; but the butcher failed to appreciate the significance of the birds still being in the air. Nor did he possess the old cowhand's knowledge of other basic, but vitally important, aspects of hunting a grizzly bear. Instead of halting and studying the situation, Copson continued to ride forward and he even failed to draw the carbine.

The bitch loped ahead, making for the dead cow. At first her tail wagged in anticipation of an interesting investigation. On reaching the cow, she caught the first warning whiff of the grizzly's scent and her tail ceased to whip back and forwards. Instead a growl, which sounded three parts whine of fear, broke from her. Copson failed to read the warning signs and continued to ride forward.

Suddenly a deep, awesome roaring snarl shattered the air and the grizzly burst into sight to protect its kill. Throwing herself backwards, the bitch whirled and fled. No less shocked by the terrifying and unexpected sight, Copson's horse reared on its hind legs. Man and bull-terrier slid backwards over the horse's rump to land on the ground, but where Copson lit down on his rump, Vic arrived feet first.

No other breed of dog equalled the Staffordshire bull-terrier for gameness and Vic did not hesitate. Giving out a staccato, somewhat high-pitched bark characteristic of its breed—and sounding out of keeping with its pugnacious nature—the dog charged straight at the on-rushing bear. Such tactics might serve admirably in the fighting-pit against another dog, but failed miserably when tried on a full-grown male grizzly bear. Lurching upright, the bear swung its right fore leg with savage speed. Before the dog's punishing, powerful jaws could close on flesh, it caught the full, shattering impact of the paw's blow. The long claws tore into Vic's body which had already been crushed by the impact and flung the dog through the air.

After disposing of the dog, without wasting any time, the grizzly made for Copson. The horse had bolted, tearing across the range and carrying away the only thing which might have saved the man's life; always assuming that the .45.75 calibre carbine, vast improvement that it was over the old "yellow boy," packed enough punch to knock down the bear in time.

Copson screamed as the grizzly reached him, desperately throwing up an arm in a futile attempt to protect his throat. Crushing jaws closed on the arm, sinking in and merciless claws raked flesh after tearing through the butcher's jacket, vest, shirt and undershirt as if they did not exist. Borne to the ground by the bear's weight, Copson struggled feebly and ineffectively during the few seconds of life left to him. Maybe during the brief seconds of agony he realized just what the old cowhand, Wilkie, meant when giving the grim warning back in town.

Snorting its rage, the bear stood over the bloody ruin that had been a man. Instinct led it to lap at the flowing blood and it tasted the saltiness of human gore for the first time. Like most animals, the bear had a craving for salt and, tasting it in the blood, tried a tentative bite at the flesh. Satisfied that the man's body offered something which the cow's did not, the grizzly laid hold of Copson's shoulder in its jaws and began to drag him towards the bushes. In a hollow not a hundred yards from where it made its kill, the bear started to feed on human flesh. Before it could take more than six bites, it heard a distant drumming of hooves. Memory stirred, giving a warning of other times such a sound reached its ears. The coming of a number of men could not be handled as had the arrival of a single individual. Unlike Vic, the bear's courage was tempered with caution and it knew when to run instead of standing to fight. Swinging away from the lacerated body, the bear faded off through the bushes and headed towards the high country. It went with a full stomach—and an awareness of the taste of human flesh.

Holding their horses to a fast trot, seven men rode towards the scene of the killings. When Daniels heard Wilkie's news, he forgot fishing. So did the doctor, a capable if irascible man who said uncomplimentary things about Copson's intelligence. In town they collected the sheriff and three more men, picked up suitable armament and rode after the butcher in the hope that they might arrive in time to save his life.

From various signs, the party doubted if they would be in time. They passed the red-bone hound bitch slinking along with terrified, rolling eyes and tail tucked up tight between her legs. Riding on, the party went by the body of the dead cow. Copson's highly-prized bull-terrier's smashed, ripped-open carcass hung on the blueberry bushes. Pushing on cautiously, afoot and holding their rifles ready for use, they found Copson—he was not a pretty sight.

"The—the bear's been eating him!" gasped one of the party.

"For God's sake get a blanket and cover it up!" another went on, face turning an ashy-grey colour.

Only old Wilkie appeared unmoved by what he saw. "I told him," the grizzled cowhand stated. "I said it wasn't a chore for an amateur."

"You told him," admitted the rancher. "Head back to town and send word for Scobie Dale."

CHAPTER TWO

I Never Needed More Than One

"I won't go with him, Mr. Zimmerman!"

More than just an ordinary objection to accompanying a customer filled Pauline Pitt's voice as she looked from her employer to the tall, lean, city-dressed figure of Ike Skerrit at his side.

"You'll go with whoever I tell you to!" Zimmerman replied, his fat, Hebraic face showing anger under its smooth, professionally jovial exterior.

"I'm not going!" Pauline insisted. "Let him find another girl."

"He wants you," the saloon-keeper pointed out.

On the face of it, Skerrit's insistence on Pauline as a companion did not appear to be worth causing trouble over. Certainly it could not be because she stood out amongst the other occupants of the room. Small, not more than five foot two in height, with honey-blonde hair piled up on top of her head, a pretty face and shapely body that the knee-long, low-cut blue dress of her kind did nothing to hide, she made an attractive picture; but there were at least two better-looking and more attractive girls in the room.

"And aims to have you," Skerrit stated, his lean, sallow face showing no expression to explain the insistence.

"Now stop your fooling and go with him!" growled

Zimmerman, shooting out a fat hand to catch her arm in a tight, savage grasp.

"No!" Pauline gasped, her face showing more than a hint of fear.

The customers of the Liberty Bell saloon in Braddock, Wyoming, watched the little scene without showing any sign of intervening on the girl's behalf. Being, for the most part, regular customers, they knew better than to come between Zimmerman and his staff. Any man foolish enough to do so rapidly found himself wishing that he had not, for Zimmerman hired two burly bouncers to back his play.

"Take your hand offen her arm, feller," said a low, drawling voice.

It seemed that the man who entered the saloon did not know of Zimmerman's way with busybodies who interfered in saloon business. Yet he also gave the impression that he might be capable of raising considerable objections to the bouncers rough-handling him.

Six foot one at least he stood and high-heeled riding boots did not account for any of it as he wore calf-long Sioux moccasins instead of the more usual foot covering of the range country. His shoulders had a width that told of strength and he slimmed down to a lean waist, with long legs, giving him the look of a fast mover. A battered black Stetson hat sat on a head of shaggy tawny hair. Underneath its brim, the face, tanned to the colour of old leather by exposure to the elements, might have been handsome but for the long triple line of scars which started at his forehead and ran down his left cheek to the jaw-bone. He wore a waist-long fringed buckskin jacket, open-necked dark blue shirt, tight-rolled scarlet bandana and washed-out levis pants long since faded from blue to a neutral grey. Around his waist hung a gunbelt which showed the unmistakable mark of a George Lawrence craftsman's work. Butt forward in a holster built for a fast low cavalry twist draw was a Remington 1871 army model single-shot cartridge pistol, .50 in calibre and exceptionally accurate in skilled hands. Bullets for the pistol, looking almost like they might be there to feed some rifle, fitted into the belt loops. Balancing against the Remington, on the left of the belt, hung a long-bladed knife, patterned on the fabled James Black bowie, in a Sioux sheath.

All in all the man looked mighty efficient and capable of holding up his end in any company. For all that, Zimmerman scowled dangerously; he had his customers to consider and, after all, it would not be *him* who tangled with the newcomer.

"Just who the hell asked you to bill in?" Zimmerman demanded, releasing the girl's arm and making a signal designed to fetch his bouncers to him.

"Way I heard it, the lady said she didn't want to go with this feller," replied the newcomer mildly, although with that scarred face he could never look mild. "Room here's got plenty more gals who'd likely jump at the chance of looking after him."

"I want this one," Skerrit put in.

"And she allows not to want you," answered the big man.

Zimmerman threw a glance around to learn what the hell might be keeping his bouncers from attending to their duty. Both were at different parts of the room and only just becoming aware of the need for their professional services. However, knowing the identity and trade of his customer, the saloon-keeper figured Skerrit ought to be able to handle the big intruder.

"Suppose I'm telling you that I'm taking her, no matter what she wants?" asked Skerrit, studying the other's armament with tolerant contempt and faint amusement.

"I'd still say that was up to the lady."

"Are you taking her part?"

"You might say that."

"All the way?" said Skerrit.

"Now me," drawled the big man, "I'd say that all depends on you."

Silence had dropped on the room and every pair of eyes but one riveted on the two men. For a moment Pauline stood staring from Skerrit to her rescuer, then she made her decision. Backing away slowly, as if moving out of the possible line of fire, Pauline drew clear of the men. She kept moving slowly across the room until reaching the rear door. Hardly daring to breathe for fear that it attracted Skerrit's attention, she opened the door and slipped through it into the night.

Concentrating his attention on the intruder, Skerrit failed to notice the girl's departure. His eyes lifted from the Remington to the other man's scarred face and grinned.

"I've seen those Remington one-shooters afore," Skerrit announced. "They're straight-shooting guns all right, but a man's only got one bullet in them."

"I've never needed more than one," the big man replied calmly.

"That's the living truth," put in one of the customers, wishing to show his superior knowledge, so speaking loud enough for as many of the room's occupants as possible could hear him. "That's Scobie Dale, the hound dog man."

As he was meant to, Skerrit heard the words and took them in. Over the past few years Scobie Dale had achieved considerable fame in Wyoming and the surrounding States. When a cougar took to killing the ranchers' livestock, or a bear went on the rampage, it had to be hunted down and destroyed. To do so called for specialized knowledge and equipment which the ranchers mostly lacked. That was where Scobie Dale came in. With his pack of trained hounds, backed by considerable knowledge of the animals making the trouble, he hunted down and killed the marauders. Doing so took courage—the scars on Scobie's face showed it could be dangerous—and an ability to handle a gun accurately; but not in the manner to which Skerrit's thoughts turned due to his own particular trade.

"Are you Dale?" Skerrit asked.

"So they tell me," Scobie replied, studying the other man with equal interest and failing to place him. While wearing a town suit, derby hat and walking shoes, the man did not strike Scobie as being a dude. Sallow of face, maybe, but not a big-city man trying to impress the rural hicks with his toughness. He did not appear to be the kind who would want to take such a minor issue as the girl's refusal with much ill-feeling.

"A man can right easy make a name by shooting down a few critters that're watching a pack of hounds," Skerrit stated and threw a glance behind Scobie. "Anyways, you don't have your hound pack along right now."

Pursing his lips, Scobie gave a low whistle; but he never took his eyes off Skerrit's face. Feet pattered on the board-walk outside the saloon and the batwing doors swung open. Moving as light-footed and alert as a brace of much-hunted buffalo wolves, a pair of dogs entered. Only one was a hound, a large bluetick with a ragged ear and a general appearance of latent, deadly power. Its coat was white with a saddle and other patches of the deep slate colour dog-breeders called blue, liberally ticked with the small, irregular-shaped black dots which gave it its name. In height the bluetick stood a good twenty-six inches and weighed at least eighty hard-muscled pounds.

Big though the hound might be, it was out-weighed by the other dog. An inch shorter than the bluetick, the second dog gave an impression of being rectangular in shape, with a firm, broad back, deep capacious chest and very power-ful couplings. Its head carried erect and alert, was broad, medium long with fairly small ears and a shortish, deep,

powerful jaws. Black in colour, with rich mahogany points
on head, brisket and lower legs, its tail docked close to the
root, the dog, a rottweiler, went a hundred pounds yet did
not look slow or awkward.

"I don't have my full pack here," admitted Scobie as the
bluetick stopped at his right side and the rottweiler halted
on his left. "But I reckon these two'll have to do."

Zimmerman's bouncers had been moving forward ready
to jump the big man, but they came to a halt at the sight of
the two dogs flanking him. Any man hawg-stupid enough
to tangle with those trained fighting dogs stood a better
than fair chance of winding up on the floor with one or the
other of them massaging his throat with its teeth. Much as
Zimmerman wanted to order his men to throw Scobie out,
his voice refused to pass the words. Anyway, the bouncers
would never obey him if he gave such a command.

Standing looking at Scobie and the two dogs, Skerrit
became aware of the girl's absence. Much as he wanted to
go after her, his professional pride refused to let him leave
if doing so gave the appearance of his having backed
down. Practically half the people in the room knew him to
be a hired gun-hand with the reputation of being a bad man
to cross. He had that reputation to consider, it brought in
much highly-paid work, so backing away from Scobie
Dale would cause a serious loss of status. No threat he
might utter could stop word of the incident getting around
and prospective employers tended to have doubts about
hiring a man who failed to back a play he started. Skerrit
had another thing to consider. After he accomplished his
mission in Braddock, he might run into difficulty from its
citizens. A practical demonstration of his ability always
served to quieten desires to apply the letter of the law to
him.

"Get the ga—" he began, starting to swing towards
Zimmerman, but halting as the rottweiler let out a low,

blood-chilling growl. "Watch them damned dogs, Dale!"

"Easy, Strike!" Scobie said gently. "Just don't make any sudden moves and they'll not fuss you any, feller."

"You get them curs out of here!" yelped Zimmerman, showing more courage than any of his customers expected.

"When I've done what I came in for," Scobie answered.

"And what'd that be?" demanded the saloon-keeper, refraining a natural tendency to gesticulate as he found the bluetick studying him with sinister intent.

"Just to have a word with the Wells Fargo agent."

Turning his head, Zimmerman looked over his shoulder. "You, Swales, come on up here and see to Dale."

A stocky man rose and walked across the room, but kept out of the firing line and halted well clear of the dogs. Being an employee of the Wells Fargo Company, he could guess at the reason for being called out.

"Was there something, Scobie?" he asked.

"I thought you knew more about that than I do," Scobie replied. "Heard tell that you've a message for me."

"Sure have. There's a grizzly gone on the rampage up Desborough way. It's already killed and part-ate one feller. Looks like they need you up there mighty bad, don't it?"

"It looks that way," admitted Scobie. "I'll be going then."

The trouble ought to have ended right then. Having work to do, Skerrit did not mind letting things drop if it could be done without loss of face on his part. However, in any crowd there can always be found somebody who wants more of a thrill than the situation presents.

"Old Scobie sure made that hired gun sing low," said Braddock's particular specimen of the thrill-seeking breed, pitching the words high enough to reach Skerrit's ears without sacrificing his own anonymity.

Cold annoyance flickered briefly in Skerrit's eyes at the words. He knew that he must now make a play against

Scobie Dale if he wished to retain his reputation for being a
real hard man.

"If you didn't have those curs along—" he began.

"They're here, mister," Scobie pointed out.

"Reckon you figure standing up for the gal's the only
way she'd look at you," sneered Skerrit. "She'd have to be
blind to take to a face like that."

"Least I wouldn't have to call on the house-man to
rough-handle her into coming with me," Scobie answered
quietly. "Which same, I'd've thought she'd be just about
the right size and heft for you to work on yourself."

For probably the first time in his life Skerrit acted without thinking. He expected his comment on Scobie's face to
rouse the other man into a rash act. Instead of reacting to
the taunt, Scobie calmly turned the tables by coming back
with a comment even more scathing.

Dropping his right shoulder forward in a manner which
caused the side of his jacket to swing open, Skerrit sent his
hand to where his Smith & Wesson 1881 Navy revolver
rode in the type of holster originally designed by Dusty
Fog* for use by a big-city detective who could not wear the
normal Western rig.† The holster pointed the revolver's
four-inch barrel to the rear and threw the butt into a position which looked awkward to eyes used to the type seen in
the range country, yet gave a remarkable speed potential
when a man learned its use. After much practice Skerrit
could boast of being something of a master at drawing
from the high-riding concealed holster.

In a flickering move Skerrit started to bring the Smith &
Wesson out of leather. He saw that Scobie was also com-
mencing a draw, but figured he could get off the first shot
—and at that range would be unlikely to miss. Even as

---

*Dusty Fog's story is told in the author's floating outfit books.
†Told in The Law Of The Gun.

Scobie's right hand turned palm out, fingers folding around the worn walnut grips of the Remington, Skerrit brought his revolver out in the special circular motion the holster required. Everything was going Skerrit's way.

Then the rottweiler cut loose with another growl, this time louder and accompanied by a tensing of his powerful muscles ready to spring. Skerrit saw the dog, heard it growl, and changed his mind. Instead of swinging the revolver into line on Scobie, he began to turn it in the big dog's direction. At the vital moment he hesitated, unsure which of the two dangers must receive first attention.

Scobie took the decision out of Skerrit's hands in no uncertain way. Only a shade slower than the other man, his Remington left the holster even as Skerrit's revolver began to swing into line. Without the dog's intervention Scobie would have died, but the respite, brief though it was, gave him his chance. Not wishing to shoot Skerrit, for he knew the terrible effect of the .50 calibre solid lead bullet he used had upon living tissue, Scobie did not cock the hammer and squeeze the hair-trigger. Instead he whipped the pistol upwards in a semicircular swing that drove the barrel under the other's jaw, gliding in a step to come within touching distance. The Remington 1871 Army single-shot pistol weighed two pounds, three ounces and lacked any delicate cylinder which might be damaged on impact, so it made a mighty effective club at close range.

Caught beneath the jaw by the Remington's eight-inch barrel, Skerrit's head snapped back. He pitched to one side, the Smith & Wesson clattering from a limp hand, crashing to the floor and lying still.

"Easy all!" warned Scobie as one of the bouncers started to reach for a gun.

Although the Remington's bore was only half an inch across, it looked a whole heap larger when one saw it—as the bouncer did—lined on his favourite belly. Even as he

spoke, Scobie swung the pistol to cover the bouncer and
end any further move on that worthy's part. Waist high, yet
lined as true as if held in a fancy Eastern target-shooter's
stance, the menace of the Remington's yawning muzzle
posed a threat only a fool would ignore.

Nor did the second bouncer show any greater initiative.
He might have taken a chance but the rottweiler turned its
attention his way and brought any moves contemplated to a
halt before they began.

"Anybody else going to object to me leaving?" asked
Scobie, twirling the pistol away.

"I wouldn't've minded if you'd never come in," Zimmerman replied.

"That's no way to get rich, turning aside good customers," grinned Scobie.

Turning on his heel, Scobie walked from the room. As
he watched the big man's departing back, Zimmerman
could feel the weight of a Remington Double Derringer
sagging his jacket pocket. If he experienced any desire to
draw and use the weapon, he managed to keep it in control. Ethics did not stay his hand, no code of honour prevented him from shooting Scobie in the back. Rather it was
the menace of the two dogs.

Although their master had left the room, rottweiler and
bluetick remained standing and facing Zimmerman and the
bouncers. A whistle sounded in the street and the dogs
turned to lope through the batwing doors. Growling a
curse, the first bouncer completed drawing his gun.

"I wouldn't do that," the Wells Fargo agent warned.
"You can bet all you own that Scobie Dale's stood where
he can draw a bead on you. Happen you even tried to shoot
that hound dog man's dog, you'd be dead afore you
squeezed the trigger."

CHAPTER THREE

So You're Working for Him

Only for a few seconds did the silence continue after the departure of Scobie Dale and the dogs. Then talk welled up as the tension snapped. While the situation did not develop as some of the crowd might have liked to see it, most of them felt they had seen enough to make conversation upon.

Being a shrewd businessman, with a top-grade working knowledge of the saloon-keeper's trade, Zimmerman lost some of his anger at Scobie Dale almost as soon as the batwing doors ceased swinging from the dogs' departure. Such an incident would have a salutary effect on the customers, bringing about a desire for discussion. In its turn, that would induce thirst and the saloon carried cures for dry throats behind its bar. What had looked like being a quiet evening now showed every sign of livening up, to Zimmerman's profit.

A moan from the sprawled-out Skerrit brought Zimmerman's eyes to him. Glancing at the bouncers, Zimmerman told them to take Skerrit into his private office. Common humanity did not dictate the order, such an emotion being foreign to the saloon-keeper's make-up. Knowing how Skerrit earned his living, Zimmerman wanted to learn, if possible, what brought the man to Braddock. A top-grade professional killer like Skerrit mostly possessed important connections, men in high places on both sides of the law, who would expect that he received every consideration.

Taking hold of Skerrit by the arms, the two bouncers raised him from the sawdust-coated floor. They showed a greater gentleness than usual when handling a customer in such a condition. Any man who received the hospitality of their employer's private office could not be treated in the manner of a drunk or a rowdy clubbed down by one of their good right arms.

After attending to Skerrit's well-being, Zimmerman looked around the room. He aimed to teach that short runt of a new girl a lesson she would never forget, and could claim to be something of an expert on doing that. However, she did not appear to be present.

"Where'd Pauline go?" he growled to one of the other girls who passed on her way to the bar.

"I don't know, Mr. Zimmerman."

Nor did anybody else. Most of the crowd had been so completely absorbed in watching the drama being played before the main doors and failed to take any notice of the main bone of contention. So Pauline's departure went unnoticed; or if any of her fellow workers saw her leave, they withheld the fact. Zimmerman's reputation as an employer was about as low as a reasonably good saloon-keeper's might be and not of a kind to induce loyalty among his employees.

"Tell her I want to see her as soon as she comes back," he growled and followed the Skerrit-loaded bouncers into the private office.

Telling the bouncers that he did not want to be disturbed, Zimmerman dismissed them. Then he turned towards the sprawled-out shape on his best and most comfortable armchair. Maybe he ought to take his chance and search Skerrit before the man recovered. Before Zimmerman could form any opinion on the propriety of such a move, Skerrit started to groan a way back to recovery. A knock at the door caused Zimmerman to turn. Jerking open the door, he glared out at the bouncer who stood on the other side.

"Figured Skerrit'd want his gun," the man said, holding out the Smith & Wesson before his employer could demand to be told why he disobeyed orders.

Taking the revolver, Zimmerman grunted what might have been thanks and closed the door again. By the time he turned, all chances of searching an unconscious man had gone. Holding his jaw and sitting crumpled in the chair, Skerrit shook his head from side to side and groaned. Zimmerman went to his desk, unlocked and opened the small cupboard at the right side and took out a bottle of whisky which normally only made an appearance when he received a visit by somebody of importance. Pouring out a liberal drink, he returned and offered it to the groaning man. Skerrit took the glass, shuddered and emptied its contents down his throat. For a time the killer sat with his head in his hands, then he looked up.

"That come from the right bottle," he said, in a slurred voice.

"Will you have another, Mr. Skerrit?"

"I've never been known to refuse."

Although not the answer he hoped to hear, Zimmerman poured out a second drink of less liberal proportions. He saw Skerrit eyeing the glass and topped it up reluctantly.

"Smoke'd go well," Skerrit hinted after downing the second drink. "Only not those rolled cow-droppings you sell behind the bar."

"I've a box of real good cigars," replied Zimmerman reluctantly, hoping he would see a return for the trouble he took.

"Trot 'em out."

With one of Zimmerman's expensive cigars smoking in

his mouth, Skerrit sank back in the chair. The saloon-keeper found his guest's unwinking stare disconcerting and decided to make a move.

"Dale left, Mr. Skerrit," he said. "With those dogs backing him, we—"

"Where's the gal?" interrupted Skerrit.

"I—I'm not sure. She wasn't in the bar-room when we carried you in here."

"Then where'd she go?"

"Out back, maybe," suggested Zimmerman. "But I've got other girls just as good and maybe better than that runt."

"I want her," stated Skerrit flatly. "Where else'd she be, happen she isn't in the john?"

"I wouldn't know. She's only been here a week or so and this town don't take any girl who works for me as a friend."

"Does she live in?" growled Skerrit, massaging his throbbing jaw. "Let me have another drink."

Generosity had never been one of Zimmerman's good points and he disliked a further dissipation of his stock. He also possessed a broad streak of caution and had no intention of crossing so dangerous a man as this professional killer. Pouring out another drink, he handed it over and watched it disappear down Skerrit's throat. Shaking his head, the killer set down the glass and returned to his questioning.

"I said does she live in?" he repeated.

"No."

"Where then—and my jaw aches too much to keep on talking unnecessary."

"She's got a room down at Mama Cochrane's place," Zimmerman replied and paused, then saw the anger furrow forming between Skerrit's eyes, so continued, "It's a small frame house around by the side of the livery barn."

"Does she know that hound dog man?"

"Not unless she met him in some other town. He's not been in here before—a man wouldn't forget him easy."

"I know I won't," purred Skerrit, touching his jaw with a gentle finger-tip. "When's the next stage due out of this one-hoss town?"

"Not until the day after tomorrow."

An uneasy sensation began to creep over Zimmerman as he considered the way in which the conversation ran. Suddenly he began to realize that more than a mere customer-girl relationship lay behind Skerrit's interest in Pauline. Being a man of some experience, Zimmerman started to draw conclusions; and did not like what he saw.

"There's no freight outfit likely to be pulling out to-night?" Skerrit asked.

"There's not one in town to go."

"How about that hound dog man, will he pull out soon?"

"I'd say 'yes' to that," Zimmerman admitted. "He's been down here after a cougar that slaughtered almost a hundred sheep from one flock. With that message from Desborough, he'll likely be pulling out real soon."

"Where'd I find his wagon?"

"I don't know."

Skerrit looked an obvious question, but Zimmerman held back from obeying it. By all the signs, the water began to rise to beyond the level of safety Zimmerman expected in any enterprise to which he lent his assistance. Sensing the other's reluctance and guessing at its cause, Skerrit took the wallet from his inside pocket. He extracted a letter from the wallet and passed it to Zimmerman. Surprise and respect began to creep on to Zimmerman's face as he read the message on the sheet of paper. It removed any lingering doubts he might have as to the advisability of helping the killer.

"So you're working for him," the saloon-keeper breathed, folding the letter almost reverently.

"You could telegraph and ask," answered Skeritt with a mocking grin.

Rising, Zimmerman went to the office door and looked into the bar-room. One of his bouncers saw him and came forward. The man proved better informed than his employer and gave the required information.

"You'll find the wagon at the livery barn," reported Zimmerman on rejoining Skerrit after closing the door. "Dale left it there while he took out after the cougar."

"I'm going out the back way, Zimmerman," Skerrit said, sliding the Smith & Wesson into its holster. "Only I've never left the office, should anybody ask."

"Sure," agreed Zimmerman without any enthusiasm.

"Keep that letter safe for me. If I run into trouble, I'd sooner not have it found on me."

Considering the contents of the letter, Zimmerman felt agreement with his guest. Nor did he care for the idea of holding on to such an important and incriminating item. Not that he went so far as to voice his opinion.

"I'll see to it," he promised, sounding less happy by the word.

"Make sure nobody's about out there," ordered Skerrit and when the saloon-keeper reported all was clear went through the rear door into the night. Before walking away, he repeated his earlier warning. "Remember now. I never left your office."

With that he strolled away, leaving a scared, worried Zimmerman to shut the door. While strolling through the deserted back streets of the town, Skerrit gave thought to the girl's possible course of actions. Every instinct gained in several years of such work told him that she would try to escape. She had shown a remarkable ability to run and slipped out of two other towns when her pursuers drew near. Knowing of his presence, and being fully aware of what he came to do, Pauline would try to leave town fast. How to do so would be her problem, unless she reached the same conclusion which Skerrit foresaw. Any man sufficiently reckless and gallant to horn in as Scobie Dale had, might be expected to carry the affair through to its bitter end. If the girl thought so, she would go to Dale. Yet she was unlikely to desert her property. At least she had not in the other two towns.

The route taken by Skerrit brought him to Mama Cochrane's small frame house before he reached the livery barn. It might be advisable to prevent the girl joining Scobie Dale and inside the house would be the place to do it. While Mama Cochrane's home did not carry the usual hanging red lamp to guide travellers to its hospitable doors, it was a "house" and in such a place Skerrit might expect a certain licence as well as the kind of assistance Zimmerman had already rendered.

"I'm coming, I'm coming!" said a peevish voice as Skerrit pounded on the building's front door. A short, fat old woman wearing a once garish but now dirty robe opened the door and peered suspiciously out.

"Is Pauline here?" Skerrit asked.

"Tried where she works?" demanded Mama Cochrane. "This ain't the sort of—"

"The law stop you running it that way?" growled Skerrit. "I remember them closing you in Caspar."

"That was because—"

"I *know* what it was because," interrupted Skerrit. "Now let's get the hell inside. I won't ask peaceable again."

During a life spent first as girl, then madame, in a variety of cat-houses across the country, Mama Cochrane had learned many lessons. She could tell the kind of man she dealt with and knew better than to stand arguing.

"I can tell by the smell that you're no john law," she

sniffed and stood aside. "Ain't Pauline down at the saloon?"

"Would I be here asking for her if she was?" growled Skerrit. The effects of the whisky had begun to wear off and his jaw throbbed again.

"Reckon not. Hell, mister, she could have come back and me not heard her, if she used the back way. I've got some nice girls here if you can't find her. One of 'em's a real Italian countess—"

"You had a German duchess in Caspar, only she'd been born in Williamsburg, Pennsylvania, it came out. Where's Pauline's room?"

"Down the back there," Mama answered. "I let some of Zimmerman's girls live in here, but keep them away from mine."

Followed by Skerrit, the woman went through to the rear of the building and along a passage with half-a-dozen doors let into its left wall. Halting before one of the doors, she indicated it as being rented to the girl he sought.

"Let's have a key," ordered Skerrit, reaching for the handle. "And don't waste any more time if you want to stay in business."

Like Zimmerman, Mama knew enough to guess at Skerrit's trade. In fact, when she found time to study the man in decent light, she recognized him and could remember certain important connections he served. The threat of putting her out of business was not an idle one; he—or rather his connections—possessed the means to do it with more permanency than the law ever managed. Dipping her hand into the robe's pocket, she produced a master key and inserted it into the keyhole. After turning the key, she twisted at the door-handle but found it did not turn.

"There's a chair jammed under the handle," she told Skerrit.

"Is, huh?" he grunted.

Dropping his shoulder, he charged the door. Twice he rammed hard into the wood and the panel splintered under the second impact. Ignoring Mama's protests, Skerrit turned and kicked in the panel. He reached through, gripped the chair that had been placed leaning so that its back held firm under the handle and after some difficulty freed it. Tossing the chair aside, he opened the door and entered a small room. In the light of the passage's lamp he looked around the room. One glance told him that he came too late. Pauline had been back, as was proved by the jammed door, open drawers in the small dressing-table, a stocking lying on the floor—and the sight of the open window. Walking to the window, Skerrit looked out. About a hundred yards away stood the dark bulk of the livery barn. Skerrit drew his head back into the room and turned to rejoin Mama in the passage.

"Get your door fixed," he said, handing her a couple of ten-dollar bills. "And forget I've ever been here."

"Sure, mister," Mama replied.

"You don't ask questions, or raise a squawk," Skerrit said. "I like that."

"Mention it to your boss," said the practical Mama. "I'm tired of being cooped up in this one-horse flea-trap town."

Skerrit did not reply. Turning on his heel, he walked back into the front hall. A pounding on a front door caused him to halt and throw an inquiring glance at the woman.

"Into my room while I see who it is," she hissed, indicating a door.

Fuming at the delay, Skerrit obeyed. He entered the woman's private room and drew his Smith & Wesson while peeking through the narrow crack he had left the door open. The knockers proved to be a trio of cowhands, all carrying a load of Old Stump Blaster internally and seeking the kind of diversion Mama supplied for a price. Impatiently Skerrit waited until the normal prior formalities of such a visit were carried out. After Mama showed her new guests upstairs, he left the room and went out of the front door. By the time Mama returned, full of sympathetic explanations and apologies for the delay, she found no need for them. Skerrit had gone.

Walking through the darkness, Skerrit studied the livery barn and wondered how he might best scout it. To go around one side and examine the front from a corner struck him as the first answer. Then he remembered the nature of the man with whom he must contend. Wherever Scobie Dale might be, there would be his dogs; the tools of his trade. To make a mistake could prove dangerous, if not fatal, when dealing with such a man.

At the rear of the big main building of the barn, Skerrit tried the door and found it unlocked. He carefully eased it open, ready to draw it shut again at the first sound of a dog's growl. None came and he stepped into the barn. To assist his customers, the barn's owner kept a couple of lanterns burning in the barn, allowing anyone who wished to collect a horse to see what they were doing. Apart from a few horses, Skerrit found he had the barn to himself. He crossed to the front window and looked out, the big main doors being closed for the night although not locked. One glance told him that he had called the play right.

Before the building stood a four-wheeled wagon of the Rocker ambulance pattern originally designed for the U.S. Army during the Civil War, and still regarded as the best vehicle of its kind in use. Scobie Dale stood at the wagon, having just completed hitching its team, with the girl at his side talking a blue-streak or Skerrit missed his guess. He could also make a reasonably accurate forecast at the nature of the conversation. Even without the stimulus of hatred caused by the hound dog man felling and humiliating him, Skerrit knew the other must die. Such information

as Pauline possessed, given out to the public, would ruin
Skerrit's employer. So she and any person to whom she
imparted even a portion of her story must die.

Bringing about the death presented something of a
problem though, as Skerrit saw in his scrutiny of the situation. While he could see the wagon well enough, the front
of the barn being illuminated as well as the interior, ob-
taining an unrestricted line of fire at the man or girl presented difficulties. Going out of the rear door and around
the side did not offer any answer. Scobie Dale's dogs,
half-a-dozen hounds and the rottweiler, stood or lay around
the wagon and would be sure to hear him no matter how
quietly he moved. Even a town-dwelling man like Skerrit
knew enough to be aware of that fact. Nor would he be any
better off if he broke a window or opened the front door. In
either case the sound would alert Scobie Dale and Skerrit
had already received one demonstration of the speed with
which the hound dog man could act.

Looking around in his search for a way out of the dead-
lock, Skerrit saw a ladder leading up to the hay loft. That
might possibly supply the answer. He walked to the foot of
the ladder and began to climb it. As his head drew level
with the two, he found that luck appeared to be with him.
During the day, hay had been brought up into the loft—
drawn by rope and pulley to the scaffold built over the
large door set in the wall for that purpose—and the door
left open. That offered Skerrit an ideal and safe way of
handling his business.

Stepping cautiously, he advanced towards the loft's
door. He slid the Smith & Wesson into his hand, cocking it
rather than chance the slight deviation in aim caused by the
pressure required to operate the double-action mechanism.
On reaching the door, he paused and looked down. Clearly
neither Dale nor the girl suspected his presence, for they
stood face to face talking. A rifle leaned close to the hound

dog man's hand against the front wheel of the wagon, but that did not worry Skerrit. Long before Scobie Dale realized his danger, or could take up the rifle, he would be dead.

"First Dale, then the girl," thought Skerrit and brought up his revolver.

CHAPTER FOUR

An Error of Ignorance

After his dogs joined him, Scobie Dale dropped the Remington back into its holster and turned to walk along the street. He grinned sardonically as he wondered why in hell he billed in upon that business in the saloon. It was always the same, let him see a girl or little feller being picked on and he had to intervene. Only on this occasion he might have been more indiscreet than in most cases. More than one man who entered into such a game wound up lying face down on the range with a bust skull and pockets emptied by the girl he tried to help.

Yet the girl had seemed to be genuinely afraid, or Scobie was no judge. It might have been her first night at such work causing her to have doubts as to the wisdom of taking employment in a saloon; but he felt that something far deeper lay behind her refusal to go with the man.

Well, the incident had ended; unless that hard-case wanted to make something more of it when he recovered. If so he would have to come after Scobie. The news about the bear demanded immediate attention. Desborough lay a good three days' journey away from Braddock and the sooner he reached it the better. Only rarely did a bear take to eating human beings, but it easily developed a taste for such salty and easily obtained flesh. When that happened,

35

a man had more trouble than plenty and then some. The sooner that bear died, the quicker the folks out Desborough way could sleep easy in their beds.

On reaching the livery barn, he found that its owner had led out his team horses and fastened them to the Rocker wagon. Before hitching the team, he went to the small shack loaned to him as a temporary kennel for his hound pack. Opening the door, he let out two blueticks, a pair of black and tan coloured Plott hounds—the tan striped with brindle lines—and a treeing-Walker, white with tan markings. All the dog hounds, and the bluetick bitch looked in the peak of condition, healthy, hard-muscled, as tireless as buffalo-wolves and without any hint of the tail-drooping fear many dogs of the day showed due to harsh, cruel training and breaking methods. Scobie stood firm in his belief that kindness—not mawkish sentimentality—beat whip, choke-collar or other such methods used by most of his kind. Anyone comparing the spirits of his pack with the usual run of hounds could not help agreeing his way paid the best results.

Allowing his hounds to roam about, Scobie led up his big riding horse. He had already removed the saddle and left it inside the wagon while visiting the saloon, so needed only to fasten the horse's hackamore to its usual place on the tailgate. Thinking back on what happened at the Liberty Bell, Scobie slid the rifle from the saddleboot. Before starting to hitch up the team horses, he rested the .50.95 Colt Lightning Express rifle against the nearside wheel. Happen that jasper from the saloon felt like making more fuss, he might not come alone and, like he pointed out, the Remington held only one bullet.

Strike, the rottweiler let out a low growl, standing facing the end of the building. Even as Scobie reached towards the butt of his pistol, he saw the small girl step around the corner. Carrying a small bag, hastily packed if the trailing sleeve of a dress proved anything, she stood looking in his direction.

"Can I come over?" she asked.

"Come ahead," Scobie offered. "Quiet, Strike. Don't worry about the dogs, ma'am—and don't try to lay a hand on any of them."

While the girl's arrival might be part of a trap, Scobie felt little concern. Happen she had companions, lurking in the darkness, ready to jump him, well the pack ought to find them first. Then let the lurkers do the worrying.

"What happened down there?" she asked, nodding in the direction of the saloon and setting down her bag.

"Not much," Scobie replied.

"Was there any trouble?"

"None that I know about."

"But Skeritt—the man who wanted me—"

"We settled things," Scobie answered. "You don't reckon he's likely to still be wanting you, do you?"

"I *know* he will be," Pauline stated. "So I've got to get out of here the worst kind of way."

"Just 'cause some jasper wants you out of a saloon full of willing gals?"

"I'm the one he wants," the girl insisted. "No matter how willing the rest."

"You know your affairs better than I do," commented Scobie.

"That's for sure," Pauline agreed. "So I'm asking you to take me with you when you pull out. You are going tonight aren't you?"

"As soon as I've hitched up the team. When a grizzly takes to man-eating there's no time to be wasted in running him down."

"Will you take me along?"

"Because you figure that feller's after you?"

"Yes."

"My pappy wasn't a smart man, but he once in a while gave me some real good advice," said Scobie. "He always used to say, 'Son, never sit in on a game unless you know just how it's played.' Which same, there's a whole lot I don't know about this game right now."

"That feller was Ike Skerrit," Pauline explained.

"So that's who he was."

"He's a hired gun, one of the best."

"So I've heard."

"Mister, if I'd gone with him, I wouldn't've come back."

"His kind only kill when there's pay in it for them, gal," Scobie stated.

"There'd be pay in it all right. He's been hired to kill me," Pauline answered and paused to hear Scobie's comments. When none came, she continued, "He's been after me for a month or more. I thought I'd shook him until he showed at Zimmerman's tonight."

"Must want you bad, to keep after you that long."

"Bad enough. I saw Jervis Thorpe kill a man."

Scobie looked long and hard at the girl. Watching his scarred face, Pauline failed to read anything but guessed that was not due to ignorance of Jervis Thorpe's identity.

"You mean Jervis Thorpe, the big-time lawyer and politician over to Cheyenne?" he finally asked.

"That's just who I mean," the girl agreed, throwing a nervous glance around her. "I know what you're going to say. That he's a fine, upstanding man, always ready to stand up for the rights of the working folks—"

"That's what you hear about him, all right," admitted Scobie. "I only met him once; come with the Governor on a cougar hunt. Vixen didn't like him."

"Vixen?"

"My other bluetick bitch. She's in the wagon there, just about ready to drop a litter. That lil bitch's a mighty fine judge of character. You reckon you saw him kill a man?"

"I *know* I saw him," corrected the girl.

While they talked, Scobie continued to work at harnessing his horses to the wagon. Yet he paid considerable attention to the girl, more than his earlier inclination had been. When Scobie first saw Pauline coming, he expected to hear the usual story that she must leave town in a hurry to avoid the man in the saloon's unwanted attentions. Only she did not have the money for the stage fare and hoped that Scobie would be gentleman enough to help out with a loan. He could not believe that the girl would spin such a tale merely to trick money out of him. It sounded just fantastic enough to be true—and yet Jervis Thorpe, whatever faults he might have, would hardly be likely to commit a murder in front of a witness.

"When was this?" he asked.

"Did you hear about the robbery of the Cattleman's Trust Bank in Cheyenne?" Pauline inquired.

"Heard about it. The boss teller was found knifed and the vault opened with his keys. The bank lost thirty thousand dollars in cash money and that much again in securities, they do tell. Are you telling me that Thorpe took it?"

"I'm only telling you what I saw," the girl replied. They stood facing each other level with the wagon box on the side nearest to the livery barn and Pauline tried in vain to read some expression on Scobie's face. "I was working at the Crystal Palace—"

"Fancy place," commented Scobie.

"You sound as if you know it."

"I've been to Cheyenne," the hound dog man admitted.

"Well, you can guess that I couldn't afford to room anywhere in that neighborhood on my pay. Anyways, I lived on the other side of town and used to walk through the backstreets to work each night. That was how I saw the killing. I had to pass the rear of the bank if I went one way.

I was going that way on the night. Well, I saw the two fellers standing talking out back of the bank, arguing or so it looked, and stopped. You can imagine what would happen to a saloon-girl who got mixed up in a fuss, no matter how innocent she might be."

"I can imagine," agreed Scobie.

"Well," the girl continued, "I stopped in the shadows. The men talked for a spell and then the teller turned. Thorpe pulled a knife—I don't know where he carried it, in that fancy walking cane maybe—and shoved it into the teller's back."

"Then took the keys?"

"Not right then. He looked around, then walked away," Pauline answered. "He even lit a cigar as he left. That's how I came to recognize him. You can just bet that I kept quiet. In fact I think I stopped breathing until he'd gone by."

"What did you do then?" Scobie asked.

"I turned and ran. Mister, I was one scared girl. Only when I reached the Palace, I found that I'd dropped my vanity bag. It must have been the shock of seeing the murder. Anyway, the next thing I knew one of the girls told me Kale Schuster had brought it in and was asking who owned it."

"Who's he?"

"He works for Thorpe. A trouble-shooter, bodyguard, call him what you like. One thing I did know. If Schuster had the bag, they must have found it back of the bank and knew I'd seen the killing. So I got out of the Palace, went back to my room, packed and caught a train."

"And you figure they've been after you ever since?"

"I *know* they have. Not Skerrit all the time, but others like him. I'd arrive in a town, take work and before I'd been there many days, there'd be somebody asking after me. About a week ago, another girl agreed to help me. She looked enough like me to make my idea work. We changed clothes and she took a stage east. I came here to work at the Liberty Bell. Only tonight Skerrit arrived."

"And you're certain he's after you?" asked Scobie.

"Would I make up a story like this just to pull the old "ticket-home" game on you?" snorted Pauline.

"Likely not," Scobie admitted. "Only it takes some believ—"

While their master and the girl talked, the dogs roamed around the wagon to investigate such interesting smells as might be found. Suddenly Song, the treeing-Walker halted and cocked his head in the air, tilting it on one side. Then the hound went bounding towards the front of the barn, looking up towards the hay-loft and making the night ring with a deep, throaty chop baying. Catching the familiar sound, the rest of the pack joined in; the bawl of the Plotts merging with the steady, coarse chop of the blueticks and all but drowning the ordinary dog-barking of the rottweiler.

Up in the loft Ike Skerrit's revolver lined at Scobie, then a sudden shock ran through the killer as he realized that the dogs gave warning of his presence. Yet they could not be aware of his presence. Although the floor of the barn had reasonable illumination, the loft lay in darkness. If he had gone around the side of the building, the dogs would have heard him easily; which was why he climbed to the loft, so as to be above them and avoid detection. Only something had gone wrong.

Skerrit had made a miscalculation when forming his plan. It was an error of ignorance, for he failed to appreciate one basic, vital fact. As a town-dweller, he had never come into contact with a pack of working hounds and so knew nothing of the treeing-Walker's special qualifications.

The thing which set a treeing-Walker apart from the rest of its fox-chasing breed was its interest in arboreal animals. Instead of being content to trail its prey along the ground, the treeing-Walker preferred to hunt creatures which climbed trees when pursued. So such a hound possessed the knack of locating its prey—or detecting danger—well above ground level. On hearing the sounds of Skerrit moving in the loft, Song gave a warning and alerted the rest of the pack; as he had done more than once when a bear or cougar took to the branches of a tree and waited in ambush.

Years of working with hounds had taught Scobie to differentiate between the various tones they used when hunting. So he needed only to hear Song's deep-throated tree chop to know where the danger lay.

Shooting out his left hand, Scobie thrust the girl aside. In the same move he began to drop to his right knee and his other hand reached for the Colt Lightning rifle. He did not move an instant too soon. Flame lashed from Skerrit's Smith & Wesson before the killer could halt his finger pressure and alter his aim. The bullet passed through the air so close that it burned a furrow in the nap of Scobie's hat before burying itself in the body of the wagon.

While not a gun-fighter, Scobie knew just what to do in such a situation. Even as he sank down with bent left leg and right knee on the ground, his fingers closed upon the small of the Lightning's butt and started to raise the rifle. From thrusting the girl aside, his left hand came across to catch the wooden cocking grip of the trombone slide mechanism. Whipping the rifle to his shoulder, Scobie lined it up to where Skerrit showed blacker than the dark outline of the loft's door and squeezed the trigger. The rifle crashed loud in the night. Automatically Scobie's left hand flicked the wooden grip back and forwards to eject the empty case and replace it with a loaded round. Skerrit shot backwards under the impact of a solid lead bullet—Scobie did not use the 300 grain hollow Express bullet for which the rifle had been designed, regarding it as a poor killer compared with the solid variety—.50 in calibre and powered by no less than ninety-five grains of best du Pont powder.

"Under the wagon, gal!" Scobie ordered as he thrust himself up and followed his hounds towards the barn, not noticing that Pauline had already disappeared underneath it.

A powerful kick from Scobie's right leg burst inwards the small pedestrian's door of the main entrance and the pack stormed through the gap. No shots greeted their entrance and Scobie went after them. Going into the barn in a fast rolling dive, Scobie lit down on the floor and twisted into the shadows behind some bales of hay. He landed with the Lightning slanted up at the loft, ready to shoot. Nothing happened. Apart from the rottweiler and hounds clamouring at the foot of the loft's ladder, he might have had the place to himself.

Still Scobie did not rise and expose himself to a possible bullet from above. In such conditions patience was more than a mere virtue, it could be the means of remaining alive.

Something splashed wetly on to the floor behind the ladder. Scobie looked up and saw a steady dribble of liquid oozing through the boards of the loft. Substituting the Remington for his rifle, he rose, vaulted over the bales and darted forward. Following their training, the pack scattered and allowed him access to the ladder. Swiftly he climbed up to the loft, yet ready to throw himself backwards and use the pistol if the need arose.

Cautiously Scobie drew himself above the level of the loft's floor and looked at the shape sprawled upon the hay. Outside voices shouted and feet began to thud as people heard the shooting and came to investigate. Scobie ignored the sounds and climbed into the loft. Still holding his Remington ready for use, he approached the shape on the

floor. While guessing at his assailant's identity, he struck a
match to verify his conclusion. One glance told Scobie that
he guessed right and also he need not fear any further trouble from Skerrit. Driving upwards into the killer's body
just under the ribs, the .50 calibre bullet cut its terrible
funnel-like way through the chest cavity and burst—almost literally—out of the back beneath the left shoulder
blade. Skerrit would have been dead an instant after the
bullet struck him.

"Like I said, feller," Scobie remarked softly. "I've never
needed more than one."

Holstering his Remington, Scobie turned and walked
back to the ladder. He left the body lying untouched and
made no attempt to take up the killer's Smith & Wesson. If
the girl told him the truth—and Scobie began to feel in-
clined to think she did—it might be advisable to have
complete proof that he shot in self-defence. Climbing
down the ladder swiftly, he reached the floor just in time to
stop his pack charging out to where the first of the investigating people approached.

"Hold them dogs in, Dale!" yelled a voice. "It's the
marshal."

Clearly Marshal Raven had more sense than come barg-
ing in on the dogs without warning. Scobie grinned bleakly
and gave an order which silenced the pack's growls. Collecting his rifle, he walked out of the barn with his dogs
around him. Raven, the barn's owner, and a deputy marshal stood by the wagon. Beyond them a growing knot of
citizens and visiting cowhands gathered, Zimmerman
prominent among them.

"What happened?" asked Raven, keeping a wary eye on
Scobie's hound pack and the big rottweiler.

At that moment Scobie realized that the girl was no-
where in sight; even her travelling bag had gone. However
he gave no sign of making the discovery and decided to let

things ride until learning more about the girl's startling story.

"I had a run-in with a jasper down at the Liberty Bell," he said in answer to the marshal's question. "Only he figured to carry it on up here."

"Heard about the fuss," Raven stated. "Fact being I was just on my way to warn you about that feller."

"He somebody special?" asked Scobie innocently.

"I figured you didn't know him," replied the marshal. "He's Ike Skerrit."

"So that's who he is," said Scobie, trying to sound suitably impressed.

"Sure. Where is he?"

"Up there in the hay-loft."

"Is he dead?"

"They don't come any deader."

Raven eyed Scobie for a long moment, then shrugged. Even in 1895 Wyoming saw enough gun play for it to be only a minor novelty. Yet there were aspects to this one which the marshal did not like. While clear of the main course of the notorious Outlaw Trail, the town had some contact with the Wild Bunch and other criminal bands. Braddock's marshal received certain unofficial additions to his civic salary for judicious closing of eyes at the right moment. One of the reasons he came to warn Scobie of Skerrit's identity had been a desire to antagonize nobody and avoid trouble in his town. Raven had been aware of Skerrit's presence in town, although not of the man's mission; but was also aware that the killer possessed some influential connections who might not want him interfering with. Yet the hound dog man also had important friends, owners of big ranches and the like. As Scobie had no equal in the business of running down stock-killers, the men behind him would take exception should he be killed. Only it seemed that the killing went the other way and Raven wanted to try to learn as much as possible so he could explain if questions were asked.

"You figure he was looking for evens?" asked the marshal.

Before Scobie could reply, he noticed Zimmerman stood well in front of the crowd which had drawn closer. So he decided to forget the girl's arrival and disappearance.

"What else?" Scobie said.

"What caused the fuss at the saloon?"

"You mean you haven't heard?"

"I'd like to hear your side of it," Raven answered.

"It wasn't much," Scobie drawled. "I saw this jasper trying to make a gal go with him again' her will and cut in. Had to club him down a mite, whch same he didn't like it and came down here after evens."

Although Zimmerman tried to will the marshal into asking about the girl, Raven proved unreceptive. The marshal glanced to where the local doctor approached and then turned back to Scobie.

"I'd best take a look at him. You said he's up in the loft?"

"He's not likely to have moved," Scobie answered.

"I may as well come with you, marshal," the doctor put in. "The county pays me to look 'em over dead or alive."

Entering the barn, Raven collected one of the hanging lanterns and lit the way up to the loft. There he and the doctor examined the body, then checked on the Smith & Wesson revolver.

"It's been fired," Raven commented.

"Looks that way," grunted the doctor. "And afore Scobie cut loose with the rifle. It's certain sure that jasper didn't start shooting *after* he was hit."

"Yeah," agreed Raven. "The hound dog man told the truth."

"I never figured he hadn't. Let's go back down so's I

can make arrangements to have this gent moved."

While waiting for the two men to return, Scobie stood looking towards the barn. Seeing the hound dog man's preoccupation, Zimmerman decided to take a chance and check on whether the girl was hidden in the wagon. It seemed unlikely that Skerrit would shoot at Scobie unless she had been present. True the killer had a fair hate for the man who knocked him down, but knew better than to indulge in a private feud when working.

As Zimmerman started to peer into the dark rear of the Rocker wagon, he heard a growl and teeth snapped scant inches from his face to cause his rapid withdrawal. Turning, Scobie looked at the saloon-keeper and his right hand brushed the Remington's butt.

"You want something, mister?"

"There's a dog in there!" gasped Zimmerman.

"You was expecting maybe a Shiras moose?" countered Scobie.

"I—I heard a noise inside and went to look," the saloon-keeper explained, making the first excuse to come to mind.

"Thanks, but my dogs can tend to my wagon," Scobie drawled, and turned back as the marshal came from the barn followed by the doctor.

"Do you want to hold an inquest, doc?" Raven asked.

"Can't say that I do. That feller's dead. We know who did it, how and why. I don't see any point in wasting Scobie's time and the taxpayer's money."

"I'll pull out then," Scobie said, grinning at the doctor amiably.

"Sure," Raven answered.

"I wish I was going with him," the doctor said as Scobie swung aboard the wagon and started it moving, the pack around it.

"Huh?" grunted Raven.

"I was talking to the only cuss here worth listening to," sniffed the doctor. "Me."

Watching the wagon depart, Zimmerman scratched his head thoughtfully. He decided that he must make a try at learning if Pauline was aboard or still in town. The man who hired Skerrit had power and pull. It would be worth the time and money spent if Zimmerman could render a service to the killer's employer.

CHAPTER FIVE

Reckon You Told the Truth

Holding his team horses to a steady trot, the hounds loping alongside and the big zebra-dun riding stallion following without fuss, Scobie Dale drove his wagon out of Braddock and followed the trail which offered easiest travelling during the first miles to Desborough.

"Mister," said the girl's voice from behind him.

While not a man given to showing his emotions, or easily startled, Scobie whipped around on the seat and surprise showed on his face. He could hardly believe his eyes, but Pauline stood at the front of the wagon. All too well Scobie knew the fierce protective nature of the bluetick bitch in the wagon. At the best, Vixen only tolerated strangers and certainly not when they entered what the bitch regarded as her private domain. Yet the girl stood behind Scobie, as large as life and unmarked or unflurried.

"How the hell—?" Scobie began.

"I've a way with dogs," Pauline answered. "Thanks for saving me, and not letting on I was around."

"I didn't know you were still around," Scobie corrected, wondering how the girl managed to get by Vixen silently and with the bitch mean with her pregnancy.

"Thought it would be better if nobody saw me," the girl explained. "So I ducked into the wagon. I'd only just got

49

friends with Vixen when the first of the folks came and I hid under your bunk."

"Which I call quick thinking," commented Scobie, and the wagon jolted over an excuse-me-ma'am* in the trail.

"Hey, easy!" Pauline warned. "You've an expecting mother in back here." She glanced back in the bitch's direction. "It'll be any time soon, or I miss my guess."

A shiver ran through the girl and Scobie realized that she must be very cold as her clothing was more suitable for the bar-room than riding in a wagon on a chilly spring night.

"There's a wolf-skin coat on the bed," he said. "Need a match?"

"I can find it," the girl answered and disappeared into the wagon. A few moments later she emerged wearing the heavy coat over her dress. Showing a shapely leg, she swung over on to the wagon box and sat at Scobie's side. "Why didn't you say I'd been with you when Skerrit came?"

"Nobody asked if you had."

"I saw Zimmy looking in the back until Vixen scared him off. Maybe Skerrit told him that he was after me."

"Or maybe Zimmerman just wanted to get you back to work."

"You still don't believe me!" Pauline snorted.

"I didn't say that," Scobie answered.

"You meant it," the girl insisted. "Didn't Skerrit coming after me prove anything?"

"Could be he wanted evens with me for clubbing him down in the saloon. A feller with his reputation wouldn't want it known that happened to him, and he did nothing about it."

"Then why else would I be in your wagon?"

Excuse-me-ma'am: a bump in the road

"Not for my good looks, anyways," Scobie said dryly.

"You're not bad looking," Pauline replied seriously. "Apart from— How did it happen?"

"A bear clawed me."

"I'm sorry."

"The bear got around to being. You can see his hide on the floor at the L Over V any time you're that way."

One of the things Scobie hated most about the disfiguration of his face was the fact that it came about partly from inexperience and particularly because of over-confidence. Early in his independent career as a hound dog man, Scobie bought one of the recently introduced Colt Lightning Express rifles. While the Winchester Models of 1873 and 1876 proved more powerful than the old "yellowboy" 1866 rifle, neither struck Scobie as having quite the punch he required. Nor did he fancy a heavy calibre Remington or Sharps single-shot, accurate at long ranges though they might be, for general hunting—he did own a Sharps Old Reliable buffalo gun that found use for special work. So he bought the new trombone slide action Colt rifle, its .50.95 calibre striking him as heavy enough and its nine-shot magazine capacity proved the deciding factor. The Express calibre rifles were an attempt to lessen the trajectory of a black powder-powered bullet's flight and increase accuracy, using a heavy charge and light bullet.

While hunting a bear, Scobie gave the rifle its first working trial and used factory Express bullets. The pack brought the bear to bay and Scobie came up to play his part. Although he held true, the light bullet shattered on the outside of the bear's skull and provoked a determined charge. Three more bullets struck the bear before Scobie decided to take more effective measures. A shot from the old Remington pistol tore into the bear's head at the last moment and tumbled it; but not before it managed to rake open Scobie's face with its claws.

After patching up his face as best he could, Scobie skinned the bear, allowing the pack to feed on some of the meat and hung the rest in a tree. Then he mounted his zebra dun and rode eight miles to the L Over V ranch house to receive more effective treatment.

What annoyed Scobie most about the affair was that it had been a black bear weighing no more than two hundred and fifty pounds which gave him the injury. After that he always loaded his own bullets, using a solid lead ball which might not have the Express' flat trajectory, but packed enough power to smash through the skull bones of any animal he had come across.

"What will you do about me?" asked Pauline, guessing that the subject of his face was distasteful.

"Take you as far as you want to go, up to Desborough anyways. What'll you do then?"

"I've enough money to buy a stage ticket down to Arizona and I can find work there."

"In a saloon?"

"Where else?" she asked defensively.

"Pull your horns in, gal," Scobie drawled. "Only if there're fellers after your hide, working in a saloon's the easiest way to lead them to you.

"A girl has to live."

"I ain't gainsaying it. Only those fellers sent after you are hunters, like me. And I know better than go looking for cougar out on the open plains. Sure one might be there sometimes, but a cougar sticks to wooded country. That's the way it lives."

"I don't follow you."

"Those fellers know you work in saloons. So they've a start to searching for you. And saloon folks talk, travel around. How long will it be afore word gets back to them where to find you?"

When it was pointed out to her, Pauline could see the

truth in Scobie's words. "But I don't know any other kind of work," she protested.

"Can't you cook?"

"Of course I can, but not good enough to make a living at it—or at least not as good a living as I can make in a saloon."

"It's your life," commented Scobie.

"If I can make enough to go East—" Pauline began.

"Thorpe can't let you stop alive, East, West, or any other place, gal."

"Then you believe me?"

"I reckon you told the truth."

"But what can I do?" groaned Pauline.

"Like I said, get work away from saloons. But you'll spend your whole life wondering when they'll find you. Why not go to the law?"

"The law!" Pauline gasped. "Thorpe has the Cheyenne marshal's office in his pocket. They'll not move against him."

"That's local law. No man, from the Governor down, has Waco in his pocket."

"Waco?"

"The United States marshal."

"How would I be able to reach him?" the girl asked.

"I might be able to help you there," Scobie answered. "Just afore he was appointed U.S. marshal, I was down on his ranch in Utah. Happen I can reach him, he'll do what he can."

Like most folks who worked in and around saloons, Pauline found little cause to trust the average peace officer who crossed her path. She had seen local lawmen bow to power and political pull, so wondered if a U.S. marshal would prove any different. With her life depending on it, she felt disinclined to take chances.

"I—I don't know," she finally said.

"Think on it, gal," suggested Scobie. "There's no rush. We can't do much until we reach Desborough. Let's hope that nobody else can do anything faster."

After the wagon departed, Zimmerman walked slowly back to the saloon. While walking, he tried to decide what might be best to do. Most likely the girl had been with Scobie Dale, hidden in the wagon and guarded by the dog. If so he should make a move at carrying out the work Skerrit had been sent to do. Which produced a problem. What had Skerrit been hired to do about the girl?

From the fear Pauline showed when Skerrit approached her she for one figured that he came to kill. Certainly his actions at the barn pointed that way. If he intended to abduct the girl, he would hardly have made the attempt from in the hayloft. True that would be his safest way of dealing with Scobie Dale, but the girl could escape before Skerrit reached the floor of the barn.

That simplified the problem. Kidnapping the girl might prove risky; but dead women were just as silent as men in the matter of telling tales. Only one thing need now be settled, finding somebody to go after and kill both Pauline and Scobie Dale. There were too many things against Zimmerman using his own men, but he reckoned something of a more satisfactory nature might be arranged.

On arrival at the saloon, Zimmerman studied the crowd. Townsmen and local cowhands could be discounted straight away. In fact the saloon-keeper could see only three suitable candidates. A tall, blond-haired young man in the company of the best-looking girl Zimmerman hired caught the eye. Something of a dandy dresser, wearing the height of current range fashion and with a low-hanging ivory-handled Colt Civilian Model Peacemaker in a fast draw holster, he looked just a mite too prosperous for an honest working cowhand. That was the trouble, the blond young man *was* too prosperous. He would not be willing to accept such a chore as Zimmerman had in mind.

Which left the other two and to the saloon-keeper's way of thinking they presented a much more satisfactory picture. Seated at a side table, they nursed a couple of schooners of beer with such care that it seemed likely they could afford nothing better nor more in the drinking line. Both wore range clothes, were tall and unshaven; and each carried a Colt in a tied-down holster, giving the impression that they knew how to use it.

Catching one of his bouncer's eye, Zimmerman brought the man to his side. Without making his interest too obvious, the saloon-keeper indicated the two men.

"Know them?" he asked.

"Don't know what they're called now," the bouncer replied. "Back in the Dakotas the one with the moustache was Packer and the other Spice."

"Are they part of the Wild Bunch?"

"Not so's to call Butch Cassidy, Harvey Logan or Ben Kilpatrick by their first names. Those pair're small time; hoss-holders and spare guns."

Not promising material to go against the man who killed Ike Skerrit, but ideal for Zimmerman's purpose. He did not want important members of the Wild Bunch working for him. If things went wrong, the leading names of the loosely knit criminal fraternity known as the Wild Bunch had friends liable to require answers to how those things happened. While the super-organized gang—with secret oaths administered on joining, pass-words, master-minded by Cassidy, Logan, Kilpatrick and a few others—did not exist outside the lurid paperback novels of the day, the Wild Bunch still packed some weight in Wyoming. Zimmerman certainly had no intention of antagonizing them; and, while the two men might occasionally be hired for menial work when members of the Wild Bunch performed a robbery, neither had such a close connection with any band as to claim its loyalty.

"Get them into the office," he ordered.

No expensive liquor and costly cigars came out when Packer and Spice entered the office. After introducing them, the bouncer withdrew and closed the door behind him. Zimmerman looked at the two men from head to foot and they studied him with equal care.

"I didn't see you drinking much out there," Zimmerman said.

"We read the sign behind the bar," answered Packer, referring to a notice bluntly declaring that credit would not be given.

"Would you be looking for work?" the saloon-keeper asked.

"Not if it's heavy toting," Spice replied.

"You don't look the heavy toting kind," Zimmerman sniffed.

"That's the living truth, mister. Me 'n' Packer's some too delicate for it."

"This chore wouldn't want some shooting done on it, nor nothing dangerous like that, now would it?" Packer went on.

"Would you object if it did?"

"Can't say as we would—happen the price's right and you're not choosey on how we go about it."

For a time Zimmerman did not speak. Doubts nagged at him, although he realized the extreme delicacy of his position. If he gave the wrong order, having the girl killed when Kale Schuster wanted her alive or *vice versa*, nobody would stop to consider that he merely acted for the best. Nor would his position be much better if he did nothing, or wired Schuster for advice. In either case the girl might escape completely and bring recrimination down on the saloon-keeper's head.

Of course if he made the correct decision, Zimmerman would find Schuster willing to listen to a request and maybe agree to it. Zimmerman's ambition was to move into a big town, so as to share in the greater profits a saloon offered in such an area. Gaining possession of such a place took more than money, which he had. Permission must be granted by the men who controlled the town; without it no saloon-keeper could open, or if he opened, show a profit. Having Schuster backing him, Zimmerman would be able to open anywhere and might even be allowed to set up in Cheyenne; with all the possibilities given by living in the State capital.

Sucking in his breath, Zimmerman reached his decision. Every sign pointed to Schuster wanting the girl dead. If the worst came to the worst, Zimmerman figured he might claim that the dead Skerrit told him that Pauline must be killed. The fact that Zimmerman held Schuster's letter requesting that every aid be granted to Skerrit would lend a ring of truth to the statement.

"I want a killing done outside town and you can handle it any way you want," he told the waiting men.

"Who is it," asked Spice, "and where?"

"Now me, I'd say let's hear how much we get first," interrupted the more practical Packer.

"One hundred—and fifty dollars each," offered Zimmerman, wanting to have the thing done for the lowest possible price.

"For a killing?" sniffed Packer.

"Hell, there'll be no risk to it. How does one-seventy-five each sound?"

"All right, for openers—eh, Spice?"

"Sure, Pack, we can always go up later."

"I want you to go after a wagon that's headed out on the Desborough trail and learn if there's a gal with it."

"And if there is?" asked Packer.

"Kill her," said Zimmerman, taking the plunge.

"She travelling alone?" Packer inquired mildly.

"There'll be a man along."

"He'll not go for us killing the gal," Spice pointed out.

"Then you'll have to kill him too," Zimmerman explained.

"On the Desborough trail?" asked Packer, still suspiciously mild-voiced.

"That's what I said," the saloon-keeper agreed.

Packer and Spice exchanged glances, then turned towards the door. "See you, mister," Spice said.

"You mean you won't do it?" yelped Zimmerman.

"For a lousy one-seventy-five each—when the man's Scobie Dale? Mister, me 'n' Spice may be close to the blanket, but we're not stupid."

"We saw the fuss in the bar and heard what the Wells Fargo man told Dale," Spice continued.

"Two hundred each," Zimmerman yelped as the men started to walk slowly towards the door. "Kale Schuster's behind this. He wants it done."

Even as he spoke, Zimmerman found himself wishing he had thought to mention Schuster before raising the price. Only the top names of the Wild Bunch might take chance on ignoring such an important man's wishes and the pair in the office did not belong in that class. Turning, they came back to the desk.

"Two hundred apiece," Packer agreed. "A bottle of whiskey and some rifle bullets. We're both out and're going to need them to handle Dale's dogs."

"Which same the store's closed up for the night," Spice continued.

"There's a box behind the bar," Zimmerman growled. "You can have them and a *small* bottle of whiskey. When you've done the job, you can have another."

"You toss money around like a man with no arms," Packer sneered. "Only we work like your sign behind the bar."

"Work best on a full stomach, which same neither of us's the money to get right now," Spice went on. "So we'd surely admire to have more'n loving words afore we ride out."

"All right, you've a deal," said Zimmerman. "Fifty dollars down and the rest when you bring me Dale's guns and the girl's clothes. What you do with the bodies is your affair."

"Bring you *all* the gal's clothes?" Packer asked.

"Sounds like it'll be fun," Spice grinned. "It's a pity we'll have to kill her afore we lay hands on her."

"How about if the gal's not with Dale?" Packer inquired, throwing a warning scowl at his frivolous partner. "The hound dog man gets on real good with Butch Cassidy."

"Leave him be unless the girl's there," Zimmerman confirmed. "Come back and let me know. That girl's got to be found."

"We'll see to it," promised Packer. "Make sure you let Mr. Schuster know how we helped."

Like the saloon-keeper, Packer was aware of the rosy future which lay ahead of any man fortunate enough to come under Kale Schuster's patronage.

Leading the way from his office, Zimmerman took the men to the counter and told the bartender to tend to their needs. After accepting the small bottle of whiskey, box of rifle bullets and money, Packer walked from the saloon with Spice on his heels.

The tall blond cowhand finished his drink and started to shove back his chair. Being aware that he carried a well-filled wallet, the girl seated at his table protested.

"You're not going, are you?" she asked. "I've room at my place—"

"Now there's a thought," he grinned. "Only I want to go for a meal first. I—sleep—better on a full stomach."

"All right," smiled the girl. "But you come back now, after you're fed and ready to—sleep."

CHAPTER SIX

A Bad Time to Give Birth

Some three hours out from Braddock, shortly after midnight, Scobie Dale brought the wagon to a halt in a large clearing and upon the banks of a wide stream. Caution dictated that he selected such a place and not only because of the girl's presence. Meat-hunting had seriously depleted the wild animal life, especially so close to a large town, reducing the numbers of deer, elk and Shiras moose to such an extent that the predatory creatures such as grizzly and black bears, cougar, wolverine and wolves turned to horses or cattle for an alternative food supply. More than one man lost his horses to prowling predators through failing to take suitable precautions.

Not Scobie. Out in the centre of a large clearing, even if the predator came with the wind blowing towards it, the pack would locate its presence and give the alarm long before it reached the horses.

"Can I help you?" asked the girl as he picked up his Colt Lightning and jumped from the box.

"You'd spoil them fancy duds," Scobie replied.

"I'll fix that if I can find my bag."

"Here's a match. You'll find a lantern hanging up inside."

Climbing back into the wagon, Pauline rasped the match on the side and lit the lantern. For the first time she found a chance to look over Scobie's travelling home and liked what she saw. She liked the neat orderliness of the interior, finding it far different from what she expected. Designed for the swift, comfortable transportation for sick and wounded men over road-less country, the Ricker ambulance offered a fair amount of room inside. Scobie had removed the double tier of beds which would carry eight wounded, replacing them with a single bunk fixed to the right wall. Four large chests were nailed to the other wall, her travelling bag on one of them. At either side of the front stood a sack of the "dog cakes" produced some thirty years before by Englishman James Spratt and now marketed all over the United States. A yellow oilskin "fish," two buckskin jackets and another heavy coat hung from the canopy supports. By the tailgate lay Scobie's Cheyenne-roll saddle, with the leader flange extending over to the rear of the cantle-board in the manner designed by Frank Meanea in the early 1870's. The bitch curled up on a mattress of burlap and straw by the bunk, watching the girl and gently beating her tail on the floor.

"Land-sakes, Vixen," the girl said as she opened her bag. "I never thought I'd need these things again."

Looking at the items of clothing taken out, Pauline wondered why she had kept them. Maybe as reminder of the life she left, should she ever tire of working in saloons. Under the present conditions she felt mighty grateful that she did not yield to the impulse and discard the garments of her pre-saloon days. Stripping off all her saloon clothes, she donned the other items. After repacking her bag, she threw another comforting word to the bitch, swung on to the wagon box and dropped to the ground.

Working on the team, Scobie threw a glance towards the girl. Then he jerked around, right hand twisting about the butt of the Remington.

"Well dog-my-cats!" he gasped, releasing the pistol.

"Aren't you the one for handing a man a fright."

"I never wore anything else while I was growing up," Pauline replied, just a touch self-consciously.

Although the man's shirt and levis pants had fitted reasonably well when she last wore them, eighteen months in a saloon had caused her to fill out and add inches to certain places so that the clothes now felt a mite snug. However, the change appeared to have made a vast improvement, if Scobie's admiring glances were anything to go on.

"When I said 'fright' I called it wrong," he told her. "Yes, sir, there's nothing more sure than that."

Pauline smiled at the words. Somehow his comment neither embarrassed nor annoyed her. Accepting it as a compliment, she looked around for some work to do. She wriggled her bare toes on the grass, taking pleasure in the sensation. Even after a year and a half her feet still felt cramped and pinched in shoes, for she never owned a pair until starting work in a saloon.

"Now what work can I do?" she asked.

"Make a fire first. There's enough wood in the possum belly to get it going. I'll tote some more in when I've tended to the horses and hounds."

Producing wood from the rawhide container nailed to the underside of the wagon bed, known as a possum belly after the female opossum's marsupial pouch, Pauline found that her old skill at fire-lighting had not deserted her. Scobie had attended to the team horses and started work on the zebra dun by the time she stood back satisfied with her work.

"Where's the coffee-pot?" she asked.

"In the first box from the back of the wagon," Scobie replied. "If you want any food—"

"I'm not hungry, but I'll cook something for you."

"Fed before I came to the saloon. Coffee's in the second box."

After lowering the tail-gate, Pauline climbed on the step and into the wagon. The first box proved to contain cooking utensils, eight dog-feed bowls and a large sack full of meat. Taking out the coffee-pot, she lowered the lid and opened the second box, finding it stocked with canned goods, a couple of parfleche bags of pemmican and other foods. Curiosity made her glance into the other two chests, the third holding clothing and the fourth a Sharps buffalo rifle, ten-gauge shotgun, Winchester Model '73 carbine, securely resting in racks on the sides, boxes of ammunition, a small keg of black powder, a couple of blocks of lead and re-loading equipment.

With female curiosity satisfied, the girl took coffee, pot and a couple of tin cups out of the wagon.

"Can you lift Vixen down?" she requested. "She looks like she's ready to go for a slow walk, only we don't know each other well enough for me to chance handling her yet."

"I'll tend to her," Scobie answered.

After lifting the bitch to the ground, he watched her amble slowly along on Pauline's heels towards the stream. When Vixen halted to perform the proposed "going," one of the Plott hounds loped over; a boisterous youngster acting in a manner most unsuitable to the bitch's current delicate condition.

"Get out of it!" Pauline yelled at the Plott. "Skat!"

A low growl rumbled in the big Plott's throat, its seventy-five pound frame tensing slightly. Next instant it skipped hurriedly aside as the coffee-pot flew at it from the girl's hand.

"You heard me!" Pauline warned. "The next'll hit you on your fool head!"

Scobie watched the by-play with a grin coming to his face. Whatever the girl might be, she sure enough knew how to handle dogs. Which was just as well happen she aimed to ride with him as far as Desborough. He did not want to spend the entire trip wet-nursing a scared female who howled for help every time one of the hound pack went near her.

On returning from the stream, Pauline set the pot on the fire. By that time Scobie had fixed the zebra dun's nose-bag on and returned to the wagon. Helping Vixen back inside, he opened the first box and took out the feed tins. Once again the girl came to volunteer her services and he asked her to put about a pound of the "dog-cake" into each tin. Opening the meat sack, he scooped out around two pounds of raw flesh into each bowl and the girl mixed it with the "dog-cake" from the sacks.

"I usually put in some green stuff," Scobie remarked. "But I ran out."

"There's some squaw-cabbage down by the stream," Pauline replied. "Shall I go fetch some for you?"

"We'll gather it comes morning," Scobie replied.

Again he found himself wondering at the calm competence the girl showed. In his experience, the average saloon girl knew practically nothing about outside life and he could not remember meeting one before capable of recognizing squaw-cabbage on a dark night.

Taking the feed bowls out, Scobie placed them down some distance away from the wagon and close to the stream, keeping them far enough apart to prevent quarrelling among the dogs. Not until he gave the word did the pack advance, but on arriving at its bowl, each dog began to eat with the gusto which told of good health.

As became the pack's strike dog, Strike was permitted to have his food close to the fire. Pauline brewed coffee and was just about to pour it out when the rottweiler lifted his head and looked in the direction from which they came. A low growl sounded from the rottweiler and immediately Scobie reached for his gun, eyes following the direction of the dog's stare.

"Best get into the wagon and hide," he told the girl. "That's Strike's man-growl. Take your coffee with you."

Obediently the girl rose and carried her cup of coffee to the rear of the wagon. She climbed inside and Scobie closed the tail-gate behind her.

"I'll put the lantern out," she said.

"Smart thinking," Scobie agreed. "I don't know who's coming, but we'd best take no chances until we learn."

Returning to the fire as the girl doused the lantern's light, Scobie laid his hand on Strike's neck.

"I hear 'em, old pal," he said. "Leave be, though."

Following its orders, the rottweiler started to eat once more; but its general attitude told him that its keen ears followed the stealthy approach of the unseen men. Farther away, the rest of the pack failed to catch the sounds and so continued to eat undisturbed.

Any doubts Scobie might have felt about the reason for the visit ended as the men came to a halt still hidden and did not make their presence known. For almost ten minutes they remained concealed, but the dog's attitude proved they were still on hand. At last Scobie felt that he should make a move.

"Speak, Strike," he whispered.

Throwing up its head, the dog cut loose with its deep bark and bounced forward a couple of steps towards the hidden men.

"Hey, easy there!" yelped a voice. "We saw your fire and just come over."

"Come on in then," Scobie answered, having once more reached for his gun as if just becoming aware of the man's presence. The hounds let out a clamour and began to move forward. "Leave it, you bunch!" he yelled and they returned to their interrupted feeding.

Keeping a wary eye on the dogs, Packer and Spice walked from the bushes and across the clearing.

"You got quick eyes and ears, friend," Packer stated. "We only just now walked up."

"The dog here let me know you were coming," Scobie replied, realizing that the other merely tried to make him believe they had only just arrived. "Don't often see men afoot out here."

"Saw your fire and figured it'd be best to make sure who it was camped here first," Packer explained. "It might have been some of the Wild Bunch."

"Would that have worried you?" Scobie asked dryly.

"It'd worry any honest man," Spice answered.

Which, although Scobie accepted the statement at its face value, did not entirely answer his question. He studied the two men and recognized their type just as easily as Zimmerman had in the saloon. Certainly they did not come into Skerrit's class if they should be hired killers. Maybe they even told the truth. Not every long-riding outlaw in Wyoming belonged to the Wild Bunch. Even within the loose bonds of the notorious association feuds ran rampant and some of its members could not tolerate others. Caution became a way of life among outlaws and the stealthy scouting of the camp might have been merely to learn if enemies used it—but the presence of the girl offered another reason for the newcomers' actions. Even while talking, both men darted glances about the camp.

"I can't offer you any food," Scobie told them. "Wasn't hungry and didn't aim to waste time cooking for myself. There's coffee in the pot happen you'd like some of it."

"That's good and neighbourly of you, friend," Packer said. "We'll just go collect our horses."

A whining yelp came from the wagon, drawing the two men's eyes in that direction and causing their hands to drift towards their guns.

"It's just one of my bitches," Scobie told them. "She's about ready to whelp-down."

"Oh!" grunted Packer. "Let's go get the horses, Spice."

In the darkness of the wagon, Pauline listened to the men and heard nothing suspicious. Then her attention was drawn to where the bitch lay on the mattress. At first Vixen lay relaxed, then she gave a grunt and the mattress rustled to the sudden constriction of her limbs. From the sounds, Pauline knew that Vixen's labours had begun and the girl wondered what she ought to do. When the whining yelp sounded, the girl knew she could not delay much longer. A further straining on Vixen's part warned Pauline she must not wait. Passing the bitch, Pauline swung over the tailgate with the aid of the rear canopy-support and landed in plain view of the two men from Braddock.

"Scobie, it's Vixen's time," she began.

Taken all in all, the bitch picked a bad time to give birth. If she had held off just five more minutes, the two men would have been out of the clearing and did not intend to return. Satisfied that Scobie travelled alone, due to their not realizing just how soon the rottweiler detected their presence, the men intended to return to Braddock with their negative report. Although dressed in the shirt and levis, Pauline still retained her saloon make-up and hair piled on top of her head in the current fashion. So the men recognized her and knew what they must do.

"Strike!" Scobie snapped, dropping his coffee-cup and sending his hand to the Remington's butt.

Although the dog obeyed the unspoken order, snarling and hurling towards the two men, it had some distance to cover and Scobie knew could not arrive in time to save his life. Despite his frivolous nature, Spice could draw a gun with fair speed; fast enough for the circumstances at any rate. Out came Scobie's Remington, his rifle lying just too far away to be of use, its hammer cocking and trigger depressing as the barrel lined. Packer's Colt had cleared leather when a .50 calibre bullet ripped into his head and threw him backwards. Under the circumstances Scobie did not dare do other than shoot for an immediate kill.

At that moment Scobie almost wished that he could trade his prized Remington for a Colt Peacemaker, which might be lighter in size and power but possessed six bullets instead of one. While his solitary bullet wiped out Packer's threat to his life, it still left the Remington empty and Spice's Colt already started to line in Scobie's direction.

Just as it seemed that nothing could save Scobie, a shot crashed from the darkness of the trees to the left of where the men emerged. Spice jerked, spun around and his revolver fell from limp fingers. Instantly the hounds came up, baying and heading towards the unseen shooter.

"Hold them back, mister!" called a voice with a Texas drawl in its tone.

"Leave him, you dogs!" Scobie shouted, and all but the younger Plott halted. "Whip!" Scobie roared. "Leave!" Firm discipline had its effect and the dog slid to a halt. Then Scobie turned to see what Strike might be doing. The rottweiler stood over Spice, but did not offer to touch him. "Come ahead, friend," Scobie offered.

Drawing back the Remington's hammer to full cock. Scobie ejected the empty case, took a bullet from his belt loops and slid it into the chamber. While doing so, he looked to his rescuer. With a smoking Winchester Model 1876 rifle in his hands, the tall, blond Texan from the saloon strolled forward.

"Howdy," he greeted. "Figured you might need some help, so I cut in. That jasper in Zimmerman's called it right about your hand gun."

"So did I," Scobie said, glancing at Packer's sprawled-out lifeless body.

"You'd best give me a match so we can see to Vixen," the girl put in before Scobie could request information as to the Texan's timely arrival.

"Happen something's wrong, I'll tend to this pair for you," drawled the Texan.

"Let's go then—say, I never asked your name."

"I wondered when you'd get round to it," smiled the girl. "It's Pauline."

"Mine's Scobie—"

"I'd *never* have guessed," interrupted Pauline. "Do you want her to whelp down in the wagon?"

"Under it'd be best."

Lowering the tail-gate, Pauline climbed into the wagon and lit the lantern. Before Scobie could move, the girl knelt at Vixen's side and examined the bitch.

"She's not broke water yet," Pauline said. "But the spasms are coming. I'll warm some milk while you get her out of here."

"Open one of the cans," Scobie answered.

"I'm sorry I yelled and came out like I did, but I hadn't heard anything to make me think those pair were after me. Anyway, we couldn't leave Vixen in the dark."

"You weren't to know," Scobie comforted her.

"If I'd only waited—but Vixen couldn't wait."

Carefully Scobie lifted the bitch and she lay relaxed, trustingly in his arms. Almost before he had raised Vixen a foot, Pauline whipped away the mattress and carried it from the wagon. By the time Scobie reached the ground, he found that the girl had the mattress in place under the wagon ready for him to place his burden down on to it. While doing so, Scobie noticed the young Texan knelt alongside one of the bodies in an attitude of having just searched it. Pauline did not give Scobie a chance to raise the matter.

"Have you anything to drape around the sides?" she asked. "She doesn't want the wind blowing in on her."

"I've a tarp in the wagon," Scobie replied. "That'll do."

Leaving the girl, Scobie went to the rear of the wagon. The Texan joined him as he entered.

"They've nothing on them to say who they might be," the young man drawled. "Can I help you now?"

A vague feeling that he ought to recognize the other kept creeping over Scobie, yet he could not place the Texan. Hard, tough, self-reliant, a shade too well dressed, the young man might be a saint,* or member of the Wild Bunch; nothing about his appearance gave any hint.

Not that Scobie wasted time in idle conjecture, being more concerned with his bitch's welfare. Rousting out the roll of tarpaulin, he and the Texan fixed it like a wall around three sides of the wagon, leaving only the area facing the fire open.

While the men worked, Pauline emptied milk into a pan, added water from the stream and warmed the mixture over the fire. Taking the warm liquid to where Vixen lay, the girl allowed the bitch to drink.

"That ought to start something," she said, rising and putting the pan aside.

So it proved. After a short time and another spasm, the water broke and soon the first puppy slid into view. Although a maiden bitch on her first delivery, Vixen knew enough to open the birth-bag, lick the puppy clean and bite off the umbilical cord from the pup's navel.

"I reckon we'd best leave her to it," Scobie said.

"You won't get any arguments from me," replied the Texan, looking just a mite peaked.

"I'll stay by her," Pauline told the men and they walked to the fire.

"You sure came at the right time, friend," Scobie remarked, determined to learn how the other came to be in the trees at the opportune moment.

---

*Saint: An honest cowhand.

"Still don't recognize me, huh?" smiled the Texan.

"Should I?"

"It was all of three years back and I've grown some since then. When you last saw me, I was wrangling hosses on Waco's spread in Utah."

CHAPTER SEVEN

A Hard Man to Convince

Thinking back to his visit to Utah, Scobie Dale tried to place the boy. Memory stirred of a tall, gangling tow-head who looked all legs and knob-bones. He trailed Waco around like a hound-dog and drank in every word the one-time Arizona Ranger and then sheriff of Two Forks County said. Three years had been a fair time, long enough for the other to change into a well-made, capable-looking young man. Yet that did not explain why the former wrangler of the BM ranch would be up in Wyoming and on hand at just the right moment.

"Remember me?" grinned the young man when Scobie did not speak.

"Flax Fannon, isn't it?" Scobie asked.

"As ever there was," agreed the Texan.

"Why'd you leave the BM and quit working for Waco?"

"I'm still working for him."

"You're a long ways from home," Scobie remarked, glancing at the girl and bitch to make sure they were all right. "Waco send you out for something?"

"Sure."

While not a man to force confidences from a chance acquaintance, Scobie was determined to get to the bottom of the matter.

"Are you here on cattle business?" he asked.

"Nope. I'm working for Waco."

"He's a rancher," Scobie pointed out.

"He's also the best damned lawman in the West," Flax replied.

"And you're working for him?"

"I'm his deputy."

"With a badge and all?"

A grin crept to Flax Fannon's face. "Waco always allowed you played them real close the vest. Nope, I've no badge along, or any other thing to prove I'm telling the truth."

"That's not like Waco's way of working," Scobie said.

"He never had a chore like this to handle before," Flax replied.

"What's the chore?"

"To clean up Wyoming and close the Outlaw Trail."

Despite himself, Scobie could not hold down a low whistle at the words. Of course the new Governor had gained his office by campaigning to stamp out lawlessness in Wyoming, but nobody expected him to do much about it once he received his appointment. It seemed that the Governor took his campaign promises more seriously than most politicians.

"So the Governor called Waco in," Scobie almost whispered.

"He needed the best," Flax replied simply. "Why'd Skerrit go after the girl, Scobie?"

"Did he go after her?" commented the hound dog man.

"You *are* careful," drawled Flax. "I've told you enough already to get me killed twice over should you mention it to maybe a quarter of the folks in Wyoming. I came up here without a badge or anything to say who I am for a damned good reason. Should anybody get the chance to search me, they won't find anything to show I'm a deputy

U.S. marshal. I reckon you can figure out why I wouldn't want it to get out."

"I reckon I can," agreed Scobie, but did not offer to explain.

"You're a hard man to convince, *Mister* Dale," Flax said, his voice changing and a harder note entering it.

As Scobie knew, a Texan only used the word "mister" to an acquaintance when he disliked the other. So the hound dog man made his decision. After all if Flax Fannon told the truth, he could be of the greatest help to Pauline. There seemed no valid reason why the young Texan should invent such a story. Should Flax be another killer on the girl's trail, then he likely would not have prevented the second man shooting Scobie.

"I'm just naturally cautious," Scobie answered. "So Skerrit was after the girl. I'm not likely to start shouting it around, now am I?"

"Reckon not," admitted the Texan, sounding mollified. "I figured something to be bad wrong when she wouldn't go with Skerrit, and was getting set to cut in when you arrived. Saw her light out of there like the devil was after her, but I thought I'd best stick around to watch your back."

"Thanks," said Scobie and meant it.

"Zimmerman had Skerrit took into the backroom after you left and I waited in the bar, figured to trail him when he came to. Only he didn't leave by the front way and the next thing I knew was you'd shot him dead."

"I reckon he was after the gal, not me."

"That's how I read it. Anyway Zimmerman came back from the shooting and looked the room over. I thought he aimed to come to me, but he hired this pair of jaspers instead."

"Are you sure of that?" asked Scobie.

"They're just a pair of no-accounts. Spent most of the

night nursing one schooner of beer, which meant they were mightly close to the blanket. He had them took into the office and when they came out gave them a box of rifle shells, a bottle of whiskey and some money. Which same Zimmerman's not a generous man, so he had hired them to do something."

"That figures," drawled Scobie, watching the Texan with interest.

"So I reckoned it might be worth my going along to see what he wanted done," Flax continued. "They went and fed first, then took their horses. Following them was easy enough, so easy I wondered if I might have been wrong. Then they stopped, back there on the rim where they could see your fire. Left the hosses and came in on foot. I followed them. You must have heard them and hid the gal—"

"That's what I did."

"Almost fooled me as well as them," grinned Flax. "That big critter's well-trained way he acted like he didn't know anybody was watching until you gave him the word."

"I always reckon if you're keeping a dog, he might as well be trained right."

"That's the living truth. I moved in one foot, hid away and watched what they did. It was the girl they came after."

"You've never been righter."

"Scobie!" Pauline called. "We've got trouble!"

Swinging away from Flax, Scobie hurried to the girl's side and dropped to his knees. One glance told him that something was wrong and he could guess at the nature of the difficulties even without the closer examination he made.

"There's one stuck in the passage," he said.

"That's what I thought," Pauline replied. "Have you any antelope grease?"

"In the wagon," Scobie answered and ran to fetch a can with an open top.

"All right, Vixen," Pauline crooned, gently rubbing the straining bitch's head. "Just lie easy there, we'll soon put you to rights."

Watched by the two men, Pauline dipped her fingers into the can and coated them in antelope grease. Asking Scobie to hold the bitch's head, she waited until he obeyed before making a move. Carefully inserting her first two fingers into the bitch's passage, Pauline felt at the tiny shape which met them. A look of relief came to her face.

"It's the right way round," she breathed.

Moving with care, she hooked her fingers behind the pup's ears so that she gripped the head. Then she gently pulled at it. At first nothing happened, but the pull, aided by Vixen's muscular spasm, freed the pup and it slid out. Weakly, but with relief, Vixen wagged her tail a couple of times and then started the work of cleaning the pup.

"I'll fetch her another hot drink," Pauline said, straightening up. "My, that's a big pup."

"Likely takes after his pappy," Scobie replied, wondering where the girl gained her knowledge of handling a whelping bitch.

"You can leave her to me again," Pauline stated. "That's two so far, let's hope the rest come easy."

"You handled that one all right," complimented Scobie.

"Thanks," the girl said dryly. "Don't get underfoot, this's no place for the men-folk,"

"I fetch a mean can of antelope grease," Scobie reminded her.

"Oh sure," she admitted in a tone which implied that might be the extent of his assistance, then smiled. "How are you on fetching coffee?"

"I can do that, too," Scobie told her and did so.

"Now if he'll get from under-foot, Vixen," Pauline said,

having cleaned her hands, given the bitch a warm drink and taken the coffee-cup, "we women can get on with our chores."

"Give me dog-hounds every time," sniffed Scobie.

"If it wasn't for us gals, there wouldn't be any dog-hounds, or fool men to chase after them," Pauline replied calmly.

Grinning, Scobie walked back to the fire. That girl had sand to burn and knew how to string words together. She would make some man a good wife and be a damned sight better off than working in a saloon. At which point he saw Flax Fannon's face and noticed that the young Texan had retreated to the fire.

"Something wrong, Flax?"

"Don't you tell anybody, but I just can't stand seeing anything being born."

"A lot of folks can't, there's no shame to it," Scobie replied. "Now me, I just can't stand the sight of looper caterpillars of bear one of them to touch me."

"Folks are funny," Flax stated, accepting a cup of coffee.

"Sure are," agreed Scobie. "Take the gal there. She allows to have seen Jervis Thorpe kill a man."

Young Flax Fannon might be, but he had learned to keep a pretty fair grip on his emotions. Only for a moment did the coffee-cup hesitate on its way to his lips and a flicker of interest cross his face. He tensed slightly and threw a glance in Pauline's direction.

"Do you believe her?" the Texan asked.

"Skerrit was after her, and those other two fellers. Which means somebody wants her dead real bad."

"Zimmerman sent those pair after her," Flax pointed out.

"But he didn't hire Skerrit," Scobie countered. "Why'd

he waste money on a top hired gun when he could have had it done cheaper closer to home?"

"There's that," admitted Flax. "Who was the feller she allows Thorpe killed?"

"The head teller from the Cattlemen's Trust in Cheyenne," Scobie replied, and saw the other's increased interest. "She says that Thorpe shoved the blade of a sword-cane into his back."

"A long, narrow blade shoved through his kidneys from behind," Flax said, half to himself. "I've seen one of them swordcane's blades, Scobie."

"So have I. Well, that's what the girl says."

"Would she be lying?"

"Why should she?" asked Scobie. "Or if she was lying to get a ride out of town, you'd expect her to pick a better one than that."

"Sure. The money and bonds from that robbery never did show up again. Did she see Thorpe take the teller's keys?"

"Allowed he just killed the teller after talking and walked away."

"Which doesn't mean a thing. Could be the robbery was done to stop folks thinking too much about the teller being killed. You know, everybody thought he'd been killed for the keys to the vault."

"It could be."

"That robbery never sat right with me, though," Flax drawled. "Killing the teller and taking his keys isn't the Wild Bunch's way."

"That's for sure," Scobie agreed. "They'd've come in with guns to hand and bandanas over their faces—and started spending the money afore now. I never saw one of them who could keep a dollar in his pocket for two long days together."

"But Jervis Thorpe—"

"It sure don't seem like his way either," Scobie said. "Schuster might kill; has killed in what passed for fair fights, but not Thorpe."

"Thorpe might if he'd a good enough reason," Flax pointed out. "And he just might have that reason."

"What'd it be?" asked Scobie.

"I've been up in Wyoming for the past six months, living like a long-rider, spending free and doing no work. Happen anybody checks on a couple of things I let slip, the sheriffs concerned know what to say. Anyways, I've got to know some of the Wild Bunch and they'll talk to one of their kind. Especially when cash's short for them and he's willing to buy the drinks. From what I've heard, I figure there's a real smart brain behind all the law-breaking in Wyoming and the neighbouring States—"

"I've read the *Police Gazette* too," Scobie interrupted.

"This's for real. That story in the *Police Gazette* sure handed everybody in the Wild Bunch a lot of laughs. Fact being, that was when I first started hearing about the Planner."

"Who's he?"

"Nobody knows. It could be Schuster, or somebody behind him. The Planner doesn't run the Wild Bunch or any of the other outfits, but he sells information to them about where to hit. Fellers I've spoke to tell how he lets them know when and where to hit and that if they follow his word, they get away without any fuss."

"That's mighty profitable for him," Scobie said.

"You don't know just how profitable," Flax drawled. "Who suffers when a bank is robbed and its vault cleaned out?"

"The banker, stock-holders—"

"And depositors," Flax finished. "Say a feller's running a business, doing fairly well and meeting his note at the bank. Then one day Butch Cassidy, the Sundance Kid, or somebody comes along and cleans out the bank. That feller loses all his savings and can't meet the mortgage note any more. The bank forecloses and a going business is sold cheap."

"To the same folks each time?"

"Nope. They're too smart for that. Each time they put a feller in to run it for them, only he makes like he's done the buying and has the deeds in his name—"

"Which same could be risky," Scobie remarked. "If the feller had the business in his name, what's to stop him selling it and running."

"A jasper called Suggit took up a general store cheap in Sheridan when the bank foreclosed on its owner after the big robbery up there. About a month later he disappeared and in about three weeks another feller showed up with papers all nice and legal showing that Suggit sold out to him. Three months passed and the Kansas City marshal's office found Suggit hanging in a hotel room."

"Suicide?"

"Everything looked that way."

"And the feller who bought the store?"

"He run into a mite of bad luck," Flax explained. "Started off well, putting good money into the bank every week. First off a bunch of drunken cowhands got to fighting in his place and did plenty of damage. Then somehow kerosene got spilled over his food. To cap it all, a wagon hauling barrels of beer to the saloon lost a wheel outside the store. Barrels crashed into its front, bust the door and windows up bad. Only then the feller's luck changed again, things stopped happening to him—and he stopped banking his takings."

"So?"

"Take the *hombre* in Gillette who took up a barber's shop after its owner lost all his money in their bank's hold-up. That feller got to be real popular, started courting a pretty lil saloon gal all sweet and loving. Gave her some mighty fancy and expensive jewellery and spent money on her. One night somebody come on him lying in a side-alley looking like a hoss trampled on his face. He allowed to have fallen off the sidewalk, only wouldn't say why he did it three or four times. The "fall" made him see the light, give up his free-handing ways. After the gal left town without any of her fancy presents."

"What's it prove?" Scobie asked.

"Taken separate, the two of them don't prove a thing," admitted Flax. "But you take them with maybe a dozen similar incidents in Wyoming, Utah, the Dakotas and Montana and things change a mite."

"Have they been happening?"

"Over the past eighteen months or more. Waco's been gathering word and he made me read reports until I thought they'd start coming out of my ears."

"And you figure this Planner jasper's behind it?"

"Near on every hold-up that's been well planned has left at least one small business on the market."

"There's nothing to say that Thorpe's mixed up in it," Scobie pointed out.

"No," agreed Flax. "But whoever the Planner is, he's a man who can learn things. A man who can come and go among the richest folks in the State. When he sells a hold-up, everything's there; the best time to hit, what law there is, the way to go to escape. That sort of information doesn't come easy—but a jasper like Thorpe could get it."

"What do you want me to do?" asked Scobie.

"The gal might have the key to the whole business," Flax replied. "Why else would they want her dead so bad?"

"If she did see Thorpe kill that feller—"

"Who'd take the word of a saloon-girl against an important jasper like him?" Flax interrupted. "He could claim that it was a pack of lies thought up by his political enemies. But suppose he is the Planner, or close to him, then he'd not want word like that even starting. Likely Thorpe knows that Waco's been called in to clean up Wyoming and, mister, nobody sells Waco short."

"Them who did soon wished they hadn't," Scobie drawled.

"Would Thorpe be any more worried about Pauline talking even if he is the Planner?"

"I think he would. The girl's story would give Waco a start. Then he'll keep on pushing and digging until he comes up with the answers. Those hired hands might spook if they heard a U.S. marshal was nosing around and a scared man'll talk. Happen Thorpe's the Planner, or works for him, they daren't chance giving Waco that much of a start."

"Just what have you in mind?" Scobie inquired, studying the Texan with admiration and interest. One way and another young Flax Fannon had grown into a real smart man and a credit to the fine peace officer who trained him.*

"Keep her with you and keep her alive until Waco can reach you. He's down in Utah, just waiting for something like this to give him a start."

"How about you?"

"I can't take her with me. It's taken too much work and money to get me in with the owlhoots and my place's among them so that I can learn everything possible ready for the big clean-up."

"Can you get word down to Waco?"

"The Wells Fargo agent at Witch Creek's working with me. He'll telegraph Waco in code and tell him everything. Happen you'll get an answer in Desborough."

*Waco's story is told in *Sagebrush Sleuth, Arizona Ranger, Waco Rides In, The Drifter.*

"That's where I'm taking the girl."

"Keep her with you if you can," Flax requested. "She may be what we need."

"How about this pair?" Scobie asked, indicating the bodies.

"We'll have to bury them and hide their gear where it won't be found. With luck Zimmerman'll think they took his money and run out instead of coming after you."

"Let's get started."

After telling the girl what they meant to do, Scobie and Flax removed the bodies for burial in the woods. On their return, they off-saddled the dead men's horses and turned the animals loose, then concealed the saddles and other gear. When playing such a dangerous game, with Flax's life at stake, they could not worry about the niceties. Packer and Spice lived by the gun, dying in a murder attempt and might have considered themselves lucky to receive any burial. With that attended to, Scobie brought all his considerable knowledge to bear in removing signs of the shooting.

"Give it a spell and nothing'll show," he said on finishing his work.

"With luck you'll have a day," Flax guessed. "Zimmerman won't start worrying about them not coming back until around noon. Then it'll take him some longer to make a move. I'd say it'll be getting on for sundown afore anybody comes out this way. He'll want to let Kale Schuster know what he's done and might not make another move until he gets his orders."

What Flax did not know was that, after hiring and dispatching the two long-riders, Zimmerman visited the Wells Fargo office with its clerk and sent a telegraph message reading, *"Schuster, Cheyenne. Salesman killed before making sale. Have arranged a replacement. Zimmerman. Braddock."*

If the telegraphist felt any surprise at the cryptic message, he hid it. A man in his position did not ask questions and learned to keep his mouth shut; especially when dealing with messages addressed to that particular source.

However, Flax guessed correctly on one point. After sending the message, Zimmerman returned to the saloon, checked its take for the night and went to bed. Although the saloon-keeper usually slept late on a morning, he was roused at nine o'clock by the Wells Fargo agent. Taking the message form, Zimmerman read the printed words and a feeling of anxiety bit at him. The message was blunt, to the point, and not one calculated to fill its recipient with joy.

"*Zimmerman. Braddock.*", it ran, "*Coming. Schuster.*"

CHAPTER EIGHT

My Father Was a Hound Dog Man

A sleepy-looking Pauline walked towards the fire in the cold grey light of dawn. Looking up from the frying-pan he held over the flames, Scobie nodded a greeting and Flax Fannon grinned amiably.

"Eight of them," she said. "One died and another needed some work but will live. I haven't touched the others, so I don't know whether they're dogs or bitches."

"They'll likely be one or the other," Scobie answered. "I don't go much on handling new-born pups for the first few days."

"You'll have to handle them," Flax pointed out. "It wouldn't be safe for you to stay on here."

"That's for sure," Scobie said. "I reckon we can fix up the wagon so Vixen'll ride comfortable, can't we, Pauline?"

"We can try," the girl replied. "My pappy always said the only comfortable ride he ever had in the Army was in a Rocker ambulance." She reached up a hand to shove a trailing strand of hair from her face. "Lord, I bet I look a sight."

"Stream's there," grinned Scobie, eyeing the girl's smeared make-up and unkempt hair. "Time you've washed up, I'll have breakfast ready."

"I'd best be riding as soon's I've fed," Flax remarked.

"You came by just at the right time," the girl put in.

Not until that moment did either man realize that the girl had been so busy with the whelping bitch that she knew nothing of their plans for her future. Flax glanced at Scobie and caught an almost imperceptible shake of the other's head, so said nothing. For his part, Scobie decided to withhold the news of Flax's position until he and the girl were on the trail. Once they started moving, he could tell her everything.

"It's lucky for me that he did," Scobie said.

"Well, I'll go and take a wash," the girl said. "I need one."

On going to the wagon to collect her towel and soap, she noticed a pair of long, sharp scissors placed handy in case the bitch failed to open a pup's bag, and not needed. Reaching up, she touched her hair once more. Four days in a wagon would ruin the work done on it and she could not hope to keep it tidy in its present length. Besides, a change would alter her appearance and might help to avoid any other man sent after her.

Walking to the stream, Pauline went along the bank until she found a deep hole surrounded by bushes. After glancing back and finding herself hidden from the wagon, she stripped naked and waded into the water. A sudden shock and chill ran through her, for she failed to realize how cold the water would be. However, after a moment she began to enjoy the sensation and bathed herself. With that done, the girl reached for the scissors. For a moment she hesitated, then sucked in a deep breath, shook free her hair and began to cut it. Using the water of the pool as a mirror, she trimmed off her hair until only short curls remained. When finished, Pauline dressed and returned to the wagon. Flax had already eaten and ridden off in the direction of the Witch Creek relay station to send word to his employer.

"It was real lucky him happening along just at the right

time," she remarked, taking the plate of food Scobie offered. "Or did he just happen along?"

"Nope. He followed that pair of jaspers," Scobie replied. "You look a whole heap better with your hair short and none of that paint on your face."

"Is that a compliment, or to have me mind my own business?"

"A compliment. Flax's a deputy U.S. marshal, although he's not wearing a badge and wouldn't want anybody to know it."

"Tell me about it while I eat. Then I'll feed Vixen. She'll be needing slops for a few days."

Watching the girl make up a sufficiently soft meal to meet the bitch's post-natal requirements, Scobie again found himself wondering where she gained her knowledge of such matters. However he did not ask at that moment, being more concerned with telling her of Flax's news and the plans made for her future.

"That's all depending on you, though," he finished. "Will you stick with me until Waco gets here?"

"Can he do anything?" she countered.

"I don't know, gal, and that's for sure," Scobie said quietly. "One thing I do know, though. Come hell or high water, he'll surely make a try. And he'll give you all the protection he can."

Listening to Scobie, Pauline found her confidence growing in the capability of the U.S. marshal. Of course she had heard much about Waco. To her generation, Waco was what Dusty Fog had been to the youngsters in the years following the Civil War. Peerless cowhand, master gun-fighter, fearless lawman of the finest kind, Waco's name rode high in all honest folk's esteem. So she felt that she could trust Scobie not to steer her wrong in the matter. If she co-operated with the U.S. marshal, she would be protected and he might even be able to remove the menace to her life.

"I'll do it," she decided. "I can work my way, do some cooking, help feed the pack—"

"That's not necessary—" Scobie began.

"It is for me," she finished. "Now go tend to your chores and leave me to get on with mine."

After feeding the bitch and chasing off such of the other dogs which gathered at the smell of the meal, Pauline left Scobie to hitch the team while she gathered squaw-cabbage and made up a fresh bed out of burlap and dried vegetation. The original mattress would be of no further use, so the girl burned it before dousing the fire.

Making a comfortable and safe nest in the wagon, Pauline asked Scobie to bring Vixen in. While he carried the bitch, Pauline transported the squirming new-born pups and put them with their mother. A satisfied smile came to the girl's face as she watched the litter gather at their mother's belly and start to feed.

"They'll do," she said.

With everything ready, Pauline climbed on to the box alongside Scobie and he started the wagon moving. The pack loped all around, running off their excess energy before settling down to the business of travelling. Looking the dogs over, Pauline asked a number of questions which again showed her surprising—considering her place of employment—knowledge. She identified each hound's breed correctly and showed interest in their working qualities.

"How'd you come to know so much about hound dogs?" Scobie asked when she mentioned the Plotts' normal ability on a cold trail.

"My father was a hound dog man back in Tennessee."

"He was?"

"Sure," the girl said and looking squarely at Scobie. "All he ever gave us was rags to wear, lean bellies and long, cold winters. That's why I went to work in a saloon."

"Don't like hound dog men, then?" he asked.

"Pappy was kind enough in his way, always happy, but he never did a lick of work when he could be out hunting his hounds. I swore I'd never make maw's mistake and get tied in with a hound-chasing man."

"You've sure kept your word," grinned Scobie.

"Look, Scobie," she said. "You saved my life and for that I'm real grateful. But as soon as this thing's over, I'm going right back into a saloon again."

"It's your life," he answered.

"It's nothing to do with your face, Scobie," Pauline told him gently. "I'm just not going to get mixed up like my maw did."

"Can't say that I blame you, gal," Scobie drawled. "Way I see it, having a woman around regular'd be nothing but grief."

"What kind of dog is Strike?" the girl asked, suddenly wanting to change the subject.

"He's a rottweiler. Got him from a German butcher down in the Dakotas. The butcher allowed they used dogs like Strike for working cattle and guards back in the old country. I don't know about that, but for a cattle-dog, he's got a nose that's almost hound-keen, can run all day and pitch right in there to fight at the end of the chase."

Scobie did not know that way back in the breed's early history, the rottweiler had been used by the German nobility for hunting wild boar. From one of the old hunting strains, Strike inherited a good nose and even as a butcher's dog the breed retained its fighting courage. Curiously, at that time in its native Germany the rottweiler had fallen into unpopularity for some reason and was very scarce—it would later become popular once more as a police and army dog. All Scobie knew was that Strike made an ideal leader for the pack and provided a dominant fighting spirit often needed in their work.

Conversation lapsed after discussing the rottweiler for a

time and the girl climbed back into the wagon to check on the welfare of Vixen and the pups. Finding everything to be satisfactory, the girl suddenly became aware of how tired she felt. What with the bitch whelping and everything, Pauline had not slept the previous night. So she sat on the bed, then lay back and went to sleep.

"Hey!" said a voice, while a hand gently shook Pauline by the shoulder. "Do you reckon you can come up front for a spell?"

Opening her eyes, the girl looked in a dazed manner at Scobie's face. For a moment she could not think where she might be, then memory returned and she sat up a touch stiffly.

"How long have I been asleep?" she asked.

"Three, four hours I'd say."

"Then it's high time I made Vixen another feed. Can we stop while I do it?"

"Reckon so. We'll stop along here a ways. There's a stream about half a mile ahead but we've all we need in the wagon. The last time I came up this way, the stream was up too high for me to cross. Maybe I'd best take the dun and ride ahead to check. If it's high, we'll save time and swing down south a ways."

"Go to it," the girl said.

"There's been no sign of anybody on our trail," Scobie told her. "But you'd best get the shotgun out and load it— happen you know how."

"I know enough not to try to stuff the shells in from the muzzle," Pauline replied.

"Happen you see anybody coming, cut loose with one barrel and I'll come running."

"Trust me for that," smiled the girl.

While the girl started to make up another meal of slops for the bitch, Scobie saddled the zebra dun, slid his Lightning rifle into the boot and mounted. With the pack following him, he rode away from the wagon. Unlike on his last visit, the stream ran fairly low. A bed of sandy gravel offered a firm footing for the team horses and bearing surface into which the wheels would not sink deep enough to bog down. Allowing the dogs to advance and drink, Scobie looked around him with interest. Just as he started to turn the dun, he saw something on the other bank which caused him to ride through the water.

On the other bank, he dropped from his saddle and looked down. His eyes had not deceived him. There on the sand, plain to see, were certain marks; a broad, roughly triangular depression, with four oval prints curving in front of it. The absence of any sign of claws told Scobie that he looked at a cougar's tracks. What caught his eye most about the mountain lion's sign was the size of the imprint. An average-size cougar left a foot mark about four inches long by four and a half wide, but the set he looked at went a good two inches larger. Unless he missed his guess, the tracks had been made not more than three hours ago.

With a bounty of twenty-five dollars on every cougar hide turned in to the Cattlemen's Association, Scobie could not overlook such an opportunity. In addition to that, Wells Fargo paid him a monthly retainer and gave him certain privileges for his services in hunting predators. Scobie always believed in honouring his obligations. Knowing the amount of damage a cougar could do among domestic stock, often killing for killing's sake, he did not hesitate. Yet he had the girl to consider.

There had been no sign of pursuit from Braddock, nor would there likely be until Zimmerman realized that the two men already sent had long passed the time when they should have returned. So Scobie figured he could leave the girl while he went after the cougar. From what he had seen, Pauline could keep the wagon moving along the trail with no trouble if he saw her across the stream. All being well, he ought to have run down, or lost, the cougar and be back with her before anybody from Braddock caught up.

Having been reared by a hound dog man, Pauline raised no objections to Scobie going after the cougar. In fact his request only strengthened her determination never again to become entangled with a man bitten by the love for trailing a pack of hunting hounds. She had already fed the bitch and cleaned Vixen's comfortable compound in the wagon. So, climbing on to the box, she started the team moving. Staying only long enough to make sure the girl could handle the team, Scobie rode once more towards the river.

The hounds still remained on the Braddock side of the water, but he rode through and called the biggest bluetick to him. By the time the dog arrived, Scobie had dismounted and stood near the tracks. Taking the dog gently by the scruff of the neck, he pushed its nose down on to the footprint. For a moment nothing happened, then the hound stiffened, its powerful body quivering and its nose thrusting deeper into the sand to suck in more of the familiar, but elusive smell. Scobie released his hold and stepped back. Throwing up its head, the bluetick let out a bugle-bawl that rang in the still air. Instantly every other dog stopped what it was doing, springing around to face the sound and charging forward. Spray flew and the stream's surface churned white as the pack crossed.

"Lay to, Bugle!" Scobie yelled. "Trail him down, boys!"

With heads down, noses snuffling to catch the first hint of their prey, the hounds gathered around Bugle as the big bluetick followed the scent-picture. Slowly at first, for sand did not hold scent too well, the pack advanced along the cougar's line. On hitting the grass, much stronger scent awaited them and their pace picked up. Loud rose the sound of the hounds' trail-bellowing and the finest orchestra in the world never made such lovely music to Scobie's ears.

Knowing he could rely on the pack to trail nothing but

the cougar, Scobie stood by his fiddle-footing and eager horse until the girl reached the stream. Although eager to get after his pack, he waited until Pauline brought the wagon safely across.

"Hey!" Pauline called. "You may need your horn."

A grin came to Scobie's face as he reached up and took the birch-bark horn from the girl. When hunting it served two purposes, to increase the range his voice would carry should he need to call in the pack and, placed to his ear, amplified the sound of their baying if they built up such a lead that he could not hear them without artificial aid. He had not expected to need the horn for running a cougar on a hot line, but felt pleased that the girl showed sufficient interest to hand it to him.

"Thanks," he said. "You're sure you'll be—"

"For Tophet's sake get going!" Pauline answered with a smile. "I know you're itching to follow those fool hounds."

"I'll see you then, gal," Scobie whooped and vaulted astride his horse.

"Men!" Pauline shouted back as he sent the eager zebra dun off at a fast trot in the direction of the hounds. A sound from inside the wagon caused the girl to turn and look. She saw Vixen trying to rise, lean head pointing in the direction of the rest of the pack's trail music. "Lord, Vixen. I thought becoming a mammy would have taught you different and better. There's no fool worse than one that wants to go hunting."

Even as she spoke, Pauline wondered just who she tried to convince. On more than one occasion her father took her out hunting and she enjoyed every minute of it. Or had she? One's ideas became blurred, recalling only the good times and forgetting the bad. Sure it had been fun to go out with her father, especially when some of the rich fellers from the valley came along with their fancy food and talk of the places they had been, but those times did not make up for cold, hungry winters, bare feet and ragged clothes. A girl would be a fool to take up with any hound dog man, even if he gave a hint of wanting her to do so.

Keeping a watch on her back-trail and seeing nothing to disturb her, Pauline continued to drive the wagon at a reasonable pace. She found little difficulty in controlling the well-trained team and after a time Vixen relaxed, for the sound of the pack died away in the distance.

Two hours went by and Pauline saw that the trail passed through a narrow, sheer-sided gorge. Knowing something of hunting, she did not expect Scobie to return for at least another hour and so kept the team moving. Suddenly Vixen, who had been lying quietly among her struggling, squirming litter, raised her head and gave a low whimper.

"What is it, gal?" Pauline asked.

A moment later the girl knew. Faintly at first, but growing louder by the second, came the sound of the hound pack. Pauline guessed that the cougar had swung around, making a looping circle. From what she could hear, the pack pressed it hard.

Then the wagon entered the gorge and its wheels and team's hooves raised a considerable racket which drowned out the sound of the hounds. Just as she reached the half-way mark in the gorge, Pauline saw something appear at the other end. With a sudden shock, the girl realized that just about the largest cougar she had ever seen was rushing along the gorge towards her.

CHAPTER NINE

The Wisdom of Not Carrying Identification

While riding his blue roan stallion along the trail towards the Witch Creek relay station, Flax Fannon met with a slight disappointment. He had hoped to find the place devoid of customers so that he could waste no time in contacting old George Caffery and having a message sent to Waco. Instead he saw that the place appeared to be doing a fair bit of business. Three horses were tied to the two-storey main building's hitching rack. Down before the barn stood a comfortable-looking buckboard with a canopy over it, tarp-wrapped baggage in the back and a pair of spirited horses harnessed to it.

Riding upon such a dangerous mission made a man develop caution and Flax wondered who Caffery's customers might be. Of course in addition to supplying fresh teams for Wells Fargo stagecoaches, the relay station offered food, drinks and accommodation for any travellers who might wish to stay there. Possibly the owners of the buckboard and horses would prove to be harmless and not connected in any way with Flax's affairs, but he did not aim to take a chance until he knew that for sure. Wyoming had a large outlaw population and many apparently innocent people possessed connections with the criminal element. Let one word or even a strong hint, of Flax's true status leak

out and he stood a better than even chance of winding up
dead.

As he approached the barn, Flax studied the buckboard's team. A man could sometimes learn plenty merely
by looking at the brand a horse carried. In this instance he
picked up little that helped. The horses bore the brand of a
ranch which specialized in raising and selling harness and
saddle animals throughout Kansas and Nebraska and even
did business in Wyoming.

Hoping to find Caffery inside, Flax rode his horse
through the open doors of the barn. Again he met with
disappointment, for the station agent was not present. Not
knowing how long he might stay, Flax decided to rest his
horse. He led the roan into a stall and set about caring for
it. While his business might be urgent, he did not aim to
neglect the horse. The time might come when he needed
his mount's speed and endurance to save his life or accomplish some task, so he did not intend to neglect its welfare.
Stripping off the low-horned, double-girthed saddle which
marked him as a Texan, Flax draped it over the inverted
V-shaped wooden "burro" by the doors, then he fed and
watered the roan. Deciding to leave the bedroll strapped to
the cantle and rifle in its boot until he knew whether he
would be stopping or not, Flax finished caring for the horse
and then walked from the barn. While approaching the station, he looked the three riding horses over. They all used
north-country saddles, looked in good condition and fast,
but their brands told him nothing significant.

On entering the large combined bar and dining-room of
the main building, Flax found it to be devoid of customers.
George Caffery stood behind the bar, a tall, leathery old-
timer with surprisingly young-looking eyes and a cheery
smile.

"Howdy, George," Flax greeted. "You're not very
busy."

"I've seen things worse and better," Caffery replied, darting a glance at the stairs leading up to the guests bedrooms.

"Who are they?" asked Flax, lowering his voice.

"There you have me," the agent replied. "Gal and a feller came in first, got here last night and booked under the name of Mr. and Miss Loxton, brother and sister from Kansas City.

"Are they?"

"There you've got me. Look enough alike to be kin. One thing I do know; they went to separate bedrooms and stayed there all night."

"Did you sit up all night peeking?" grinned Flax.

"Nope," grunted Caffery. "I don't need. Put her in the room over mine. It's floor creaks something fierce. Happen she'd left, or he'd come in, I'd've heard 'em no matter how quiet they moved."

"How about the other two?"

"Came in about an hour back. Names're Elmhurt and Laverick."

"What are they?"

"Not range country stock, that's for sure. Dressed like drummers but they don't have any sample-bags along and they're a couple of hard-lookers."

"Where are they now?" Flax inquired, darting glances around.

"Went up to the room they took," answered Caffery. "Claim to have rid over from Braddock to pick up the east-bound stage."

After throwing another cautious look around, with particular emphasis on the entrance to the stairs leading up to the first floor, Flax saw nothing to disturb or alarm him and so got down to business.

"How soon can you send word to Waco?"

"Just about as soon as you give it to me," drawled Caf-

fery, face showing no interest even though he knew that
Flax was only to contact the U.S. marshal by telegraph
should he have vitally important news which could not be
sent in any other manner.

Keeping his voice down, Flax told Caffery all that had
happened in Braddock and of his meeting with Scobie Dale
the previous night. For all the emotion Caffery showed, the
young Texan might have been discussing the time of day.
However, Flax noticed the old-timer's slight tensing and
knew Caffery did not underestimate the potential value of
Pauline's story.

"I'd trust Scobie Dale, was I you," Caffery commented
at last. "If he reckons the girl speaks true, you can near on
count on it."

"It could be the start Waco wants," Flax replied. "I
reckon it's worth sending word to him about it."

"Yep," agreed the agent. "I'll get the message off. But
if Schuster get to know where the g—"

At that moment a sound drifted from upstairs. Feet
thudded on bare boards and approached the stairhead,
while male voices talked. Turning towards the stairs, Flax
thought he saw a flicker of something black as if a piece of
cloth swung momentarily into sight.

"What kind of dress was that gal wearing this morning?" he asked.

"A black skirt and white blouse," Caffery replied, following the direction of the other's gaze.

The heavy feet slowed down, as if their owners came on
a sight which surprised them. One of the men upstairs
started to say something and stopped again before he finished or the listening pair in the bar could make out one
word from another. Then the feet began to sound again,
coming down the stairs.

"That gal was standing on the stairs just now," Flax
breathed.

"Listening?"

"I'd say trying to. Only she went back up as soon as she heard those two jaspers coming down."

"Reckon she heard anything?"

"We held our voices down and I don't reckon she heard much. Nothing we've said'd mean anything to her, unless—"

"Yeah," said Caffery dryly. "Unless her and her brother aren't what they look to be."

Before any more could be said, the two men reached the foot of the stairs and entered the bar-room. Flax looked the pair over with a quick, all-embracing gaze. Both equalled his height, with heavy builds that hinted of strength. Like Caffery claimed, they wore the style of clothing favoured by most travelling salesmen; yet they lacked the air of bonhomie most drummers cultivated as an aid to selling their products. The black-haired jasper carried a Forehand & Wadsworth revolver thrust into his waistband, while his sandy-headed companion wore a shoulder holster or Flax missed his guess.

Cold eyes looked Flax over with none of his pretence at casual disinterest. However, the two men did not speak but went to a table and sat down.

"Bring over a bottle and glasses, mister," called the black-haired man.

"I'll be right there, Mr. Elmhurt," Caffery answered.

Grinning a little at the manner in which Caffery introduced the two men, Flax turned back to the bar. One of the things Waco taught him was to wait and allow the other side to make first move in such a situation. Maybe he had been mistaken, occasionally a man's eyes did play tricks on him, and Caffery's guests might be completely innocent. For all that, Flax felt sure that he had seen the two men somewhere. As Caffery carried the whisky bottle and glasses around the bar and towards the table, Flax remembered. Unless he sadly missed his guess, he had seen the two men—or somebody mighty like them—in Zimmerman's saloon the previous night.

"Hey, cowboy," called Laverick. "How about joining us for a drink?"

"Not right now, thanks," Flax replied, turning towards the speaker. "I've got to tend to my hoss first."

Maybe nothing lay behind the invitation other than a desire to be friendly. Or it could be a prelude to the offer of a game of cards, in which Flax stood no chance of winning. The pair might be no more than card sharks looking to pick up some easy money while waiting for their stage. Yet there was another explanation; the pair could remember him and want to pump him about his reason for pulling out of Zimmerman's saloon on the heels of the long-riders. Whatever the reason, Flax did not intend to take chances. Setting his hat right on his head, he walked by the seated men and out of the building.

"You gents want anything for a spell?" Caffery asked.

"Nope." Elmhurt answered after a glance at Laverick.

"I'll go tend to my work then," said the agent, and walked from behind the bar.

Entering the room which held his telegraphic equipment, Caffery sat at the desk and reached for his sending key. After writing down the gist of Flax's news and request for information, the old-timer unlocked the desk drawer and took out a cipher-disk. This consisted of two concentric disks, one smaller than the other. Letters, word pauses and other information marked around the edge of the larger disk corresponded with signal numbers on the circumference of the other. By checking the disk, he could copy the entire message down. While simple to use, the code could only be broken by long, tedious calculations, unless one possessed the cipher disk.

During the War, Caffery served in United States Military-Telegraph Corps and achieved the reputation for being the fastest, most accurate sender of coded messages ever to receive pay from the Quartermaster's Department, under which his outfit came. Nor had his old skill deserted him. Deftly his fingers rattled out the message, which would be passed on until reaching the U.S. marshal down in Utah and be decoded by him with the aid of a corresponding cipher-disk.

While the room in which Caffery housed the female guest might possess some advantages, for studying the movements of suspected persons, the agent clean forgot that he had placed her brother immediately over the telegraph office. Nor did the room above offer such effective —or defective, depending upon how one regarded the matter—flooring to give warning of what went on within its walls.

Auscultation, listening to sounds from within the human body, had brought about the need for the stethoscope which Laennec invented in 1819. The man calling himself Loxton put such an instrument to a vastly different use as he knelt on the floor of the room above the telegraph office. Pressing the ivory-surfaced head of the small, flattened bell against the floorboards, he held the large, flat disk at the other end of the metal tube to his right ear.

"He's sending a message, Norah," Loxton said.

Even sprawled upon her brother's bed, clad in a plain white blouse and black skirt, Norah Loxton exuded a sensual attraction. Black hair, taken back in a severe bun at that moment, framed a beautiful face somewhat marred by coldly calculating eyes—not that most men would notice them, until too late. Although designed to avoid it, the blouse could not hide the fullness of her bosom as it rose in a magnificent swell over her slim waist. Nor could the plain lines of the skirt conceal the sweeping curves of her hips or the full shapely power of her legs. Five foot eight in height, Norah Loxton possessed the looks and figure to turn heads in any company, no matter how she dressed.

"Can you read it?" she asked.

"Pass me that pencil and notebook," her brother replied, holding out his hand without removing his ear from the stethoscope.

Six foot tall, Wilfred Loxton offered much the same attraction for women that his sister held for men. His handsome, regular features bore a family resemblance to the young woman, but without her strength of will. Although well-built, his body conveyed a hint of softness. His jacket lay at the head of the bed. It, like the rest of his clothing, was costly and of the latest Eastern fashion.

Placing the offered notebook on the floor, Loxton began to rapidly mark down symbols. After making only a few marks on the paper, his face took on a puzzled expression and he pressed his ear more firmly on to the upper disk.

Rising from the bed, Norah went to the window. Even with only her brother present she moved in a feline, sensual manner calculated to draw approving male glances and disapproving sniffs from women less endowed with feminine charms. She looked down from the window and watched Flax Fannon walk from the main building and make for the barn.

"Now who are you?" she said to herself, studying the Texan. "No ordinary cowhand, that's for sure. You and the agent were on too close terms for that. The question is, who do you work for? Well, if I can't get you to tell me, I'm not the girl I know I am."

"It's finished, Norah," Loxton said, coming to his feet and dusting the knees of his trousers with exaggerated care. "But—"

Before he could finish, the girl had advanced and taken the notebook from his hand. She looked down at, to her, a meaningless collection of numbers instead of written words.

"What's this?" she hissed.

"The message."

"You're sure?"

"Damn it all, Norah—?" Loxton began.

"All right, Wilfred," she purred. "I know you're good for something besides wheedling information from women. This is in code. Can you break it?"

"Given time, I could," he answered coldly, taking the paper.

"Then make a start at it, dear. If it's anything to do with that saloon-girl the sooner we know the better."

"And if it isn't?"

"Anything that's important enough to be sent in code has a saleable value one way or another," Norah replied and walked towards the window. "Oh no! What the hell are those fools playing at?"

The last part of her speech came inadvertently, caused by seeing Elmhurt and Laverick leave the building and head for the barn. Knowing the two men, she could guess at what they intended and a feeling of fury filled her. Since first learning of Schuster's interest in Pauline Pitt, Norah had sought for the girl and put much effort into locating her. While not entirely sure of why Schuster wanted Pauline, Norah's guess came pretty close to the truth. Learning that Pauline was working in Zimmerman's saloon, Norah sent Elmhurt and Laverick to check on the story while she and her brother followed up another lead.

Seeing the two men walk into the stage station that morning handed Norah a surprise. Fortunately they gave the agent an acceptable reason for coming and had even sense enough not to let him see they knew her. In her room, after the men came up to the one they rented until the arrival of the east-bound stage, she listened to their reason for leaving Braddock. Hard questioning drew out all but one essential fact. The men told Norah of how Scobie Dale clubbed Skerrit and later killed him, also that Pauline disappeared. While they mentioned Zimmerman sending off the long-riders, neither spoke of Flax Fannon leaving on Packer and Spice's trail. If her hired help noticed Flax, they attached no importance to his departure.

While Norah might be ignorant of Flax's interest in the affair, she did know that more than pure chance brought him to the relay station. Seeing him arrive, she decided to learn, if possible, the nature of his business. Creeping downstairs, she tried to overhear Flax's conversation with the agent and by its low-voiced manner guessed that it must be important. Perhaps she might have learned something had not Laverick and Elmhurt chosen that moment to leave their room. On hearing them, Norah turned and started back up the stairs. Only just in time she silenced Laverick's greeting with an angry gesture.

Maybe the Texan's presence had nothing to do with the business in Braddock, in fact she could see no reason why it should. However, he came to the relay station for something and learning what it might be could prove interesting. The one thing she did not want was for her hired help to go bursting in with their heavy-handed methods until she could try her own way on the Texan.

"Get the bags down to the buckboard," she told her brother, picking up the vanity bag from the bed and starting for the door. "We may not have to pull out, but if we do, it will be in a hurry."

With that she left the room. Loxton did not waste time. While he might not like her way of addressing him, he admitted that she was the brains of the family and rarely steered them wrong. Swiftly he packed the notebook and his belongings into the travelling bag, went to his sister's room and found that she had already made ready for leaving. Carrying two bags, he started downstairs.

After Caffery left to send the telegraph message, Laverick and Elmhurt sat in silence for a time. Then Elmhurt glanced at the door, listening to the tapping of the key.

"That Texan was in Braddock last night," Elmhurt commented.

"Yeah, and come here to send a message to somebody," Laverick went on.

"Who'd he send it to?"

"Let's go ask him."

"Maybe we should ought to tell Norah first," Elmhurt said.

"He might be saddled and rid out before we can," Laverick answered. "Let's go get him and make him talk. We might learn something."

"What'll Norah say?" asked Elmhurt.

"I'm getting just a mite sick of her and all she has to say," Laverick replied. "If we learn something, it won't matter what she says."

After finishing the message, Caffery first locked up the cipher disk and then burned the message sheet, crumbling its ashes into powder. Before he could leave the office, the telegraph began to click out his signal and a routine message came in to demand his attention, preventing him from leaving and noticing the departure of his guests.

At the barn Flax went to his horse first and made sure that it had everything it needed. Collecting his bedroll and rifle, he was about to leave when the two men entered. They acted in a casual manner, one going to either side of the door and each showing interest in anything but the young Texan. If anything, they made it appear too casual; although Flax gave no sign of noticing that as he walked towards them.

As Flax came level with the door and started to pass between them, Laverick withdrew his attention from the harness hanging on the wall, pivoted and threw a hard-looking right fist at the Texan's head. At Flax's left, Elm-hurt spread out arms ready to grab him as he reeled under the impact of Laverick's blow. The two men moved with skilled precision, obviously having practised their tactics. Against an unsuspecting man, the attack worked with dev-astating, simple ease and rendered the receiver incapable of making anything more than a token defence.

Unfortunately Flax was not unprepared. Even as Laver-ick struck, Flax swung up and chopped forward with the barrel of his rifle. Instead of striking flesh, Laverick's knuckles met with hard steel and he let out a howl of pain. Before Flax could make another move, however, Elmhurt reached him and he felt his arms pinned to his sides by the other's grasp.

"Do something, Lav!" howled Elmhurt as Flax strug-gled to escape from the hold. "Don't leave it all to me!"

Surging and trying to free himself, Flax dropped the bedroll but retained his hold on the rifle. Carrying it by the firegrip, he could neither use it as club nor firearm, with his hands pinned down. Laverick heard his companion's yell and sprang forward a backhand smash to Flax's face with all the power of his uninjured left arm. Again he drew back his fist, meaning to drive it into the Texan's face. Thrusting in with his high-heeled range boots, Flax dragged both himself and his captor forward. Up swung his right leg, jabbing the boot into Laverick's belly and shov-ing him backwards. However, Flax knew he must free his hands; and figured he knew just about the most effective way of doing it.

Down whipped Flax's raised leg, to drive back into Elmhurt's shin. The pain inflicted by the backwards kick was far higher than the mere bare impact could hope to achieve. Like all cowhands, Flax wore spurs; large ro-welled and with a number of points rising from them. Such an item served a useful purpose, even though the points had been blunted so as to inflict only a reminder, not punishment, when used on his horse. Blunt or not, the spurs sent a shock of agony biting into Elmhurt and caused him to relax his hold on Flax's arms. Not much, but enough. Giving a surging heave, Flax freed his arms. Then he drove backwards with the rifle, sending its metal shod butt plate into Elmhurt's groin. Again the blow did not carry his full power, but served its purpose. In addition to jackknifing its recipient over, it allowed Flax to slide his hand back from the foregrip, over the frame and close his fingers around the small of the butt.

Catching his balance, Laverick grabbed for his gun. Flax's left hand replaced his right on the foregrip, his right forefinger entered the rifle's trigger-guard and the remaining three passed through the loading lever. Held hip-high, he threw a bullet into the chamber and the menacing double click ended Laverick's move half-completed even without the grim vocal warning which accompanied it.

"Hold it!" Flax ordered, moving into a position where he could cover both of the men although that put him with his back to the open doors of the barn.

Just a moment too late, Flax saw the shadow behind him. He started to turn, ready to shoot or strike; and did neither. Had a man been there, he would not have hesitated. Seeing the girl, even though she had her arm raised to attack him, he hesitated. Around and across whipped the girl's hand, driving the leather wrapped, lead-loaded billy against the side of Flax's head. She aimed under the brim of his shoved-back hat and landed true. Blackness engulfed Flax and he collapsed to the ground without a sound.

"Get him inside!" Norah ordered.

"I'll kick his g—!" Elmhurt began and moved forward to do so.

"Do as I say!" the girl hissed.

Sullenly and reluctantly Elmhurt halted, then obeyed. Inside the barn, the two men searched Flax thoroughly and efficiently; checking the tops and soles of his boots, the inside of his belts and the sweat-band of his hat among other places. Displaying just as good a knowledge of where papers or other items might be hidden, the girl went over the rest of Flax's property. At that moment the wisdom of not carrying identification showed. If Flax had anything to prove his connection with Waco, those three efficient searchers would have found it.

"Nothing!" the girl said at last. "You damned fools! I could have learned all I wanted from him if you'd left him to me."

"Can't you now?" asked Laverick.

"He saw me, knows I hit him. Do you think he'll forget that?"

"Could be he doesn't know anything about the girl," Elmhurt pointed out.

"He knows something about something and it might have been profitable to learn what!" the girl snapped. "Dump him in an empty stall, then get the horses. If Dale took the girl with him, we'll find her at Desborough—and if we do, for the Lord's sake let me handle things, will you?"

CHAPTER TEN

Paula's Mistake

Lying on the branch of a large flowering dogwood tree, the big tom cougar woke and raised its head to listen to the sound of hounds baying. At first it ignored the sound, having heard a similar noise on more than one occasion due to its habit of raiding ranches to pick up a meal of its favourite food, horsemeat. When the baying drew closer, the cougar rose and adopted a tactic which paid good results on other occasions. Gathering itself, the cougar sprang from the branch, curving through the air with its long tail serving to keep it balanced. It lit down with barely a sound some forty feet from the tree and went loping away at an easy mile-devouring trot.

First of the pack, by a narrow margin, the treeing-Walker reached the flowering dogwood. From a firm scent picture, the line went to nothing as the cougar bounded upwards on deciding to rest in the tree; but that failed to puzzle the experienced hound. Leaping up at the trunk, the white and tan hound smelled where the cougar struck and cut loose with his tree bellow only to have it falter off as he realized that the prey no longer was up the dogwood. Independent natured animals like the rest of the pack would never accept another hound's summing-up of a situation and not until each one of them tested the tree did they halt their treed music.

Following up at a fast trot, Scobie heard the clamour, read its message and smiled grimly. No cougar in its full health would remain up a tree on hearing the approaching hounds. Not until tired and hard-pressed would it climb and stay put. Nudging the dun's ribs with his heels, he urged it on at a better speed so as to guide the pack on to the line should they need it.

Before their master reached them, the hounds started to spread out with their noses to the ground, snuffling and questing as they cast around for the line lost at the tree. Nothing but the cougar's scent mattered to the hounds; a cottontail rabbit burst from beneath a bush and passed inches in front of Belle, the second bluetick bitch's nose, without her even raising her head from the ground. A deer's scent met Song, the treeing-Walker's nostrils, and he snuffed it away as of no importance to a cat- and bear-hunting hound.

Fanning out, the pack cast with deadly precision. Even as Scobie came into sight, Dick, the second of the Plott's, slammed to a rigid, stiff-legged halt. His tail went up in a sabre curve and as unmoving as if made of steel. Throwing back his head, he shattered the suddenly silent woods with his open bawl to announce the rediscovery of the trail. Gathering fast, the remainder of the pack stuck down their noses; not even needing their master's exhortation to lay to Dick. Each hound caught the sought-after scent-picture; but with a difference. Before reaching the tree, they followed a line already three hours cold and crossed by other animals. On joining Dick, the pack found a fresh scent-picture which told them that their prey ran only a short distance ahead.

Even had he been some distance away, Scobie would have known that his pack ran a hot scent from the different tone of their voices. Excitement tinged the bugle voices of the blueticks, showing also in the baying of the Plotts and treeing-Walker. Only Strike ran mute, not adding his barking as he conserved his wind to enable him to carry his heavy frame along in company with the hounds. Away tore the pack on the cougar's line; bounding through bushes, over rocks, sliding down slopes and charging gallantly up others. All the time they made the air ring with their wild trail music, a sound which stirred the blood and caused more than one man to neglect his family just to trail the hunting hounds.

Ahead the cougar increased its pace as the sound of the hounds drew nearer. On three other occasions a taste for horse-flesh caused it to be hunted and it escaped the following dogs with little difficulty. Only this time a highly-trained pack ran on its trail; dogs bred and reared for hunting bear or cougar, wise to every trick their prey might play.

A wide, shallow stream barred the cougar's way. No obstacle for the mountain lion, like the jaguar to the South, did not fear to enter water. However, on this occasion it did not go in. Instead it left the ground in a smooth leap, covering some twenty-five feet to land on top of the eight-foot high bank at the far side of the stream. Once before it had used such a trick and completely fooled the trailing hounds.

Not more than two minutes later, Scobie's pack arrived at the spot where the cougar took off from. Only for a moment did the leading hounds hesitate. Then Bugle, oldest and most experienced of the blueticks, hurled himself into the water, splashing through, gathering himself and leaping up the bank. Fighting his way to the top, Bugle found the cougar's track and his bawl brought the other hounds over. In only a short time the hounds reached the top of the bank and struck the trail, although the same trick baffled half-trained curs and lost them.

Hotter grew the scent and faster moved the pack, their voices giving Scobie as clear a picture of what happened as if he rode with them instead of a good half a mile behind. Many a fox-hunting man—especially if he came from England, where the craze for an even pack led Masters to strive for hounds of equal size, weight and colour—might have laughed at Scobie's collection of hounds; but not for long. While there might be differences in size, colour and appearance between the blueticks, Plotts and treeing-Walker—not to mention the chunky, dock-tailed rottweiler —the group ran as a pack and held their pace to that of the slowest member. Long experience had taught the pack the folly of one hound pushing on ahead of the rest. While such a trick used against a fox might result in nothing worse than a sharp bite, it could prove fatal when the prey was a bear or cougar.

Not until they came into sight of the cougar did the pack show any signs of breaking its tight formation. Scobie heard the blueticks' voices change to a steady chop, as did the Plotts' ringing tones and the treeing-Walker's turkey-mouth singing gave final confirmation that the pack now ran their prey instead of needing to use their noses. Beneath his legs, the zebra dun quivered and fiddle-footed in its eagerness to break into a gallop; it too recognized the change in the hounds' tones.

"Damned if the gal's not right," Scobie grinned as he patted the horse's neck. "There's nothing more foolish than man, hoss or hounds that'll run to hunting. All right, you hound-trailing fool, get moving."

Given permission, the dun lengthened its stride and broke from a trot to a slow gallop. Despite the increased speed of the horse, the hounds drew ahead. Over that kind of terrain not even the cat-footed, country-bred dun could live with the pack once they started running their prey on vision and breast-high scent.

The cougar's flight turned from a fast lope to a gallop as the pack once more closed on it. Like all the cat family, a mountain lion was built for highly concentrated bursts of speed rather than a continuous fast pace, yet it could hold a gallop far better than most of the feline species. Hard-pressed by the hounds, it might have taken to a tree, but none of a suitable kind appeared as it ran through more open country than previously.

Ahead of the cougar rose a high, sheer wall of rock; a veritable haven of safety if only the cougar could once reach it. No hound would be able to climb the sheer face, while the cougar was well able to do so. Tensing its powerful body, the cougar prepared to make one of those high, sailing leaps for which its kind were famous.

Bursting ahead of the rest of the pack, with the inborn speed of its fox-hunting ancestors, the treeing-Walker flung itself towards the cougar. The big tom heard the rush of feet and snap of jaws. Putting off its leap, the cougar twisted around and slashed at the approaching hound. Long, sharp claws slid from their sheaths and gave the mountain lion's feet their deadly armament, reaching forward to tear into flesh.

Desperately the treeing-Walker halted its rush and curved its body aside. It yelped as the claws barely raked its rump, but escaped with only a minor scratch. However, Song had achieved his purpose in breaking off the cougar's leap for a vital moment. Instead of continuing its attack, the cougar whirled and jumped for the face of the cliff. Hampered as it had been, the mountain lion could not attain its full height and struck the wall well below the limit of safety. Its claws found cracks in which to dig and it began to drag itself upwards. Bursting through the pack, Strike flung himself upwards and his jaws clamped hold of the cougar's down-hanging tail. Pain and the hundred-pound weight of the rottweiler hanging on its tail caused the cougar to lose its hold on the wall and it tumbled backwards.

Strike knew better than to hang on once he felt the cougar falling. Opening his jaws, the big dog landed and threw himself to one side as the snarling, spitting cougar came down. Tail lashing from side to side, ears clamped down tight against the sides of its devil's mask face, the cougar lit down on its feet and slashed savagely at the raging hounds around it. Wisely the dogs kept their distance. Unlike Copson's bull-terrier, those hounds knew caution and would close in only to help another member of the pack should it get into difficulties.

Much as the cougar wanted to scale the cliff, it could not do so. Each time it tried to turn, one of the pack sprang forward and forced it back on to the defensive. Letting out a hissing snarl, the cougar charged, built up momentum as the pack scattered and bounded high into the air to sail over the waiting rottweiler's head. Strike reared on to his hind legs, chopping savagely but unavailingly and almost fell over backwards in his attempts to twist around and get after the leaping cat.

Urging his horse on at the best possible speed over the rugged country, Scobie could visualize what happened by the sound of his pack's voices. He knew of the mêlée at the cliff face and heard the sounds which told him that the cougar ran again. Twice more the cougar turned to fight, as he could hear from the growls, excited yelping and deep-throated barking of the rottweiler. Only when the prey stood its ground did big Strike give voice.

Turned from the safety of the cliff, the cougar sought for a suitable tree in which it might climb to safety. It failed to find one, or, when the right kind of tree came along, was prevented from climbing by the proximity of the pack. For over two hours the chase went on, from the hounds first striking the trail to when the fleeing cougar approached the Braddock-Desborough trail. Through all that time the hounds and cougar either ran or fought without a pause. Yet the chase had not been exceptionally long as such things went. Harried by the pack, the cougar swung along the trail. Ahead lay the open mouth of a gorge and the cougar headed in that direction with the intention of climbing one side or the other. Too late it found its way blocked by an approaching wagon.

High on a rim a good half-mile behind the pack, Scobie drew the lathered but still eager dun to a halt. He saw the cougar enter the gorge and to his horror noticed the approaching wagon. Finding itself trapped between the wagon and the pack, that big tom cougar would attack the thing it feared least—and it had lived on a steady diet of horse-meat. Even if the cougar did not attack the horses, its appearance before them would throw them into a panic. Either they would bolt, or try to turn back on their tracks, possibly wrecking the wagon and almost certainly crippling themselves.

Even as he started the dun running in a desperate bid to reach the scene in time, Scobie remembered that the girl should be armed. In fact he saw her reaching down to pick something from the side of the box. Loaded with nine buckshot balls, each .32 in size, the ten-gauge shotgun ought to prove accurate enough to halt the cougar even in unskilled hands. At the worst, the roar of the shot ought to scare the cougar and make it turn even if the spreading missed it. Scobie hoped that the girl would have sense enough to take some kind of aim and not fire blindly, endangering, or maybe killing some of the pack.

While the Colt company made some extravagant claims for the accuracy of their Lightning rifles—although no more so than published by the other fire-arms manufac-

turers about their products—Scobie knew that he could not
dismount, take aim and shoot with any expectancy of hitting the fast-running cougar at such a long range. Luck and
skilled sighting might combine to give him a hit; but he did
not dare chance that.

Of course all would be well provided the girl showed as
much as a slight competence with the shotgun.

Suddenly, and shockingly, Scobie realized that the girl
had not brought up the shotgun. Although still a good way
off, Scobie could see the thing she held did not have the
squat bulk of the twenty-inch twin-barrelled Greener shotgun. Instead she held his Winchester carbine; a good gun,
accurate at short range provided the one behind it knew
how to handle it properly. However, the Winchester fired
only one bullet, not a spreading cloud of nine balls.

When telling Pauline to take out his shotgun, Scobie
never intended for her to use it. The squat Greener possessed considerable deterrent value when lined at a human
being. Anybody who saw the yawning twin barrels would
think twice before coming too close to the person behind
the gun. Unfortunately, a cougar could not reason in such a
manner.

Reaching for his horn, Scobie prepared to yell advice
and at the same time kept his horse running at top speed. It
seemed to him that the girl panicked, for she rose to her
feet and leapt out of the wagon even as the horses became
aware of the approaching cougar.

"Blast and damn all fool wo—!" he began.

On seeing the cougar charging down in her direction,
Pauline did feel scared; but it was the kind of fear which
put direction and speed into her movements, not blind
panic. She needed only one glance to know that neither
hounds nor Scobie could arrive in time to halt the cougar,
so everything depended on her. And she wanted badly to
succeed. Without her along, Scobie would have left the

wagon on the far side of the distant stream, safe from the
hunted cougar. She drove his home into the danger, inadvertently but done just the same, and must save the team
horses if she could.

Bending down, she lifted the carbine from where it
rested against the side of the wagon box. It held a full
magazine of bullets, with one in the chamber and safety-
catch applied. While raising the little gun, Pauline realized
she would not be able to shoot accurately from her present
position. Already the two horses sensed their danger and
acted restlessly. Swiftly she booted home the brake and
looped the reins around its handle. Then she rose and sprang
from the box. On reaching the ground, Pauline dropped to
her left knee and swung the carbine up. Nestling the butt
against her shoulder, she sighted as her father taught her
and touched off a shot.

The .44 calibre bullet struck the cougar in the head,
somersaulting the big tom over so that its body slid along
the ground for some feet before coming to a halt. Having
been delayed by the cougar ascending a steep incline which
they could not manage, necessitating a detour that took
some minutes, the pack had not been pushing the cougar
too closely in the latter stages of the chase. By the time
they arrived, with Strike in the lead, the cougar lay dead.

As soon as she shot, Pauline rose. Waiting only long
enough to see that she did not need a second bullet, she
applied the carbine's safety-catch once more, put the
weapon on the ground and sprang to the horses' heads. She
ignored the pack as it swarmed about the cougar and gave
her attention to calming the horses. Being steady, reliable
animals, the team horses made little fuss once they realized
that the danger had passed and the girl found no difficulty
in calming them.

"Are you all right?" Scobie asked, bringing his horse to
a halt and jumping down.

"Sure," she smiled.

"When I saw the carbine, I thought—"

"I figured that if I had to shoot, I might as well hit something with the bullet," she told him. "Which same, I never took to using a shotgun, it's rough as hell on the shoulder."

CHAPTER ELEVEN

Desborough Becomes a Point of Interest

"How's it feel now, Flax?" asked Caffery, removing the wet cloth from around the Texan's head.

Seated on the edge of the relay station agent's bed, Flax Fannon reached up his hand to touch the swollen, discoloured lump on the side of his forehead. He winced and removed the fingers hurriedly.

"Hurts like hell," he replied.

"Happen it'd been a mite further back, on the temple, it wouldn't be hurting you now," said the old-timer. "That was a hell of a crack she gave you."

"Yeah," grunted Flax. "I felt it for a spell." He shook his head in an effort to clear the dizziness which filled it. "Where'd they go after she hit me?"

"I was in the telegraph room and didn't hear them leave, it being at the back of the house and made so that it keeps noise out. Time I came outside, they were topping that rim about a mile off on the Braddock trail."

"Braddock?"

"That's the way they headed. Why'd they jump you, boy?"

"I'm damned if I know."

"From what I saw, they'd searched your duffle—"

"Searched me, too," Flax drawled. "But it wasn't to

120

steal anything, they left my money in my pockets. Those two jaspers were in Braddock last night. Maybe they saw me there and thought I'd followed them. Wanted to know who I was, most likely."

Having some considerable experience as a Wells Fargo employee, an explanation presented itself to Caffery.

"Could be the gal, her brother and those other two planned to hold up a stage from here and that's why they got so jumpy when you showed up."

"Is there any shipment coming through that'd be worth going to so much trouble to rob?"

"Not that I know of," admitted Caffery. "Mind though, the company don't spread word around when there is. But a feller with eyes and ears gets to know the signs, and I've not seen any."

"I can't see those four meeting up here just to pull a stick-up on a stage that might not even give them eating money."

"Or me," Caffery agreed. "A bunch of down-to-the-blanket long-riders might, but not folks with as much money as the gal and her brother had."

"They were all in it together," Flax said. "Otherwise why'd she jump me?"

"Could've thought you was trying to rob the other two," suggested Caffery. "Which I don't believe, either."

"If she'd thought that, she wouldn't've run," Flax answered. "And she hit like she'd done it afore. How long is it since they pulled out?"

"Getting on for an hour."

"Then I can catch up with—"

"You'll stay on here for a spell!" interrupted Caffery. "Waco told me to look out for you and I'd be doing it real good happen I let you ride out of here while you're still as wobbly as a new-born calf."

"I feel all right," objected Flax.

"You don't look it," grunted Caffery. "It'll be three to one when you run up against 'em and you can't handle it the way you're fixed right now."

"You could come along."

"Don't be *loco*. My place's here and you know it. I've this place to run."

Flax nodded a reluctant agreement. Before sending him upon the dangerous mission, Waco repeatedly told Flax to follow Caffery's advice. At that moment, much as he wanted to go after the woman's party, Flax knew he was in no condition to do so. Clearly the quartet did not want him around them and might make their objections in a more definite manner next time. When a man tangled in a gunfight, especially against possible odds of three to one, he needed to be completely fit and not feeling the effects of a brutal blow to the head.

"I'll rest up for a spell," he said. "That hoss of mine'll catch up on them easy enough as long as they stick with the buckboard."

"That's the most sensible thing you've said since I found you in the barn," Caffery replied. "Did you stop to think they might not've headed for Braddock. Even with the buckboard, they can cut across country out of sight and come back on to the Desborough trail."

"Sure they could," agreed Flax. "When I'm rested up, I'll head for Braddock, but I'll watch for signs that they left the trail. Could be whatever they're doing, they're going to Braddock to do it."

"Sure, and got spooked when they saw you and re- membered you from there, not knowing what you wanted."

"Or who I might be," finished Flax, standing up. "I bet they're sure wondering about that."

•   •   •

For the tenth time in the past hour Elmhurt turned in his saddle and studied their back trail. As on each other occasion, he gave the same report.

"No sign of him."

"I'm not surprised after the way I hit him," Norah answered, handling the buckboard's reins with quiet competence. "There's the Desborough trail ahead. Once on it we can make up some of the time we lost going towards Braddock."

After leaving the Witch Creek relay station, Norah had insisted that they went in the opposite direction to Desborough and found a place upon which her party would leave little or no sign of their departure before starting to swing back in a half-circle that kept them out of Caffery's buildings. She felt that the Texan would waste time in visiting Braddock first, should he come after them either for revenge or some other reason.

"Who do you think he was?" Loxton asked. "The Texan, I mean."

"That's funny," purred Norah. "I thought you might mean him."

"Who was he?" her brother insisted.

"How would I know?" she snapped. "He'd nothing on him to say."

"Could be a long-rider," Laverick suggested. "You don't often see a cowhand that handy with a gun, wearing a rig like he does, or toting over a hundred dollars in cash."

"That's true," Norah admitted. "But he could be a peace officer—"

"Without a badge?" her brother put in.

"If he's working undercover he wouldn't have one," she replied.

"Might be a Pink-eye," Elmhurt said.

"He might, although Pinkertons don't hire many Texans. Not knowing who he is was the reason I stopped you robbing him. I can talk my way out of knocking down a man I thought was trying to rob you, but not if you'd emptied his wallet."

Elmhurt sniffed as he recalled the girl's angry objections to his attempt at robbery. Once she explained her reasons, he could see that she acted for the best. Wanting to change the subject, he asked.

"Do you reckon the gal's with Scobie Dale?"

"From what you told me, the saloon-keeper did," Norah replied.

"We don't know he sent those two long-riders after the girl and Dale," her brother protested.

"If it comes to that," Norah replied, "we don't even know that it's worth our while trying to find her."

"But you said—"

"I know what I said!" Norah interrupted her brother, seeing the interest which showed on the faces of their two companions. Neither Elmhurt nor Laverick knew why they sought out the girl and she did not intend them to find out. "Mr. Laverick told us that Zimmerman gave the two men money and rifle shells. If they were going after Scobie Dale, they wouldn't want to get too close. With luck we'll get the answers in Desborough."

"Maybe me and Jack ought to push on ahead," Laverick suggested.

"And what?" asked Norah.

"Get to Desborough, see if the gal's with Dale—"

"Then make a hash of it as you did with that Texan?" sniffed Norah. "We'll go up together. That way I'll know all the time what's happening."

She would also, although she did not mention it, be in a position to prevent her employees from trying to make use of the information she obtained. While admitting that the two men proved useful on occasion, she did not trust them too far.

"Shall we try to catch up with Dale on the trail?" Loxton asked.

"He's a good start on us, but if we should, we'll see what we can do," his sister answered. "The longer he goes without trouble, the less likely he is to expect it. So we'll not rush after him."

At about the same time as Norah stated her views to her companions, the bartender in Zimmerman's Liberty Bell stood looking at a quartet of men who entered the saloon.

Two of the four wore range clothes, with low-hanging, tied down holsters carrying Colts which rode just right for the hands that never strayed far from the butts. Medium-sized, broad-shouldered, one of the pair looked to be middle-aged and might have been an ordinary working cowhand apart from that significant gunbelt. The second stood taller, wore dandy clothes which cost more than any honest cowhand could afford. Handsome, his face held an arrogance and truculence that told a story to eyes which knew Western men. Studying the two, the bartender concluded that if their faces had not been on "wanted" posters it would be because of lack of proof rather than strict adherence to the law.

The third member of the party was a tall, gaunt Indian. Lank black hair trailed from under his battered U.S. Cavalry campaign hat, hanging around a scarred, vicious face. He wore cast-off white man's clothing, filthy and ill-fitting, with a long-bladed Green River knife in a fancy Sioux sheath at his belt, and had moccasins on his feet. Even before the Indian reached the bar, he gave the bartender a whiff of stale sweat and general dirt that warned the other not to get too close.

Although clearly with the other three, in fact giving the impression that he led them, the fourth newcomer did not have the look of a hard-case range country man. Five foot nine inches at most, he possessed a width to his shoulders

that hinted at strength. A costly white Stetson sat on his
head, yet his face did not show the usual open-air man's
tan. He wore a town suit, vest, frilly-bosomed shirt and
bow tie—and a gunbelt with a pearl-handled Colt Lightning double-action revolver butt forward for a cross-draw
at his left side. Unless the bartender missed his guess, that
belt and Colt were far from being decorations.

"Four whiskeys," ordered the young man, trail-dirty and
showing signs of hard travelling as did his companions.

"I can't serve no In—" the bartender began.

"Joey Stinks here's no Injun, bardog," the young man
interrupted. "I'm telling you so."

Which meant, as the bartender well knew, that any objections would be treated as calling the speaker a liar.
Casting a glance to where a sawn-off ten-gauge rested on
the shelf beneath the counter, the bartender wondered at his
chances of reaching it. Then he saw the mocking grin on
the young man's lips and knew what he faced. That young
cuss wanted him to make a move so as to be able to draw
and shoot. Like many of his kind, he craved the prized
name of killer and did not care how he came by it.

"Let it ride, Kid," ordered the smallest man and, to the
bartender's surprise, the young jasper obeyed. Then the
speaker looked at the bartender. "Put up the four drinks and
then go tell your boss I'm here."

"Zimmerman's in the office," the bartender replied,
pouring out the drinks and tipping a more generous mea-
sure than usual into each glass as he found a quartet of
disconcertingly cold eyes watching his every move.

"Then go get him," the young man said. "Mr. Schuster
don't like to be kept waiting for the hired help."

"Don't rush yourself, Ned," the other Westerner went
on. "Any time in the next ten seconds'll do."

The bartender did not need the added advice. As soon as
he heard the name of the small man, he started to move.

People who crossed Kale Schuster had a way of running into bad luck. Besides, Zimmerman left strict orders regarding the arrival of Schuster.

"I'll go tell him, Mr. Schuster," he said.

"Leave the bottle," the young man called.

"Put it back behind the bar," Schuster corrected as the bartender hesitated. He looked at the young man and went on, "That one drink'll do you, Tonopah. And don't let Joey Stinks have any more, we may need him."

Hearing the name, the bartender felt a wave of relief run over him. Kid Tonopah bore a name as a proddy killer, the kind who made trouble just as an excuse to throw down on a man. That other hard-case would be Jack Sage, rumour had it he and Tonopah worked together. Yet such was the power of Kale Schuster that Tonopah, looking just a mite surly, did not repeat his demand for the bottle to be left behind.

Never had the bartender seen his employer show such agitation as he did on hearing that Kale Schuster waited to see him. Telling his bartender to fetch Schuster in, Zimmerman spent the waiting time taking out his best whisky bottle and cigars.

"I wasn't sure how soon you'd be here, Mr. Schuster," Zimmerman said as the other entered. "If I'd known I—"

"Could have put out banners with BRADDOCK WELCOMES KALE SCHUSTER on them," the other replied dryly.

Despite his awe at coming face to face with the almost legendary Kale Schuster, Zimmerman felt just a shade of an anti-climax at finding the other to be so short a man. Not that the saloon-keeper aimed to put the thought into words. Any man who could wield such power over Wyoming's criminal element must be something real special in the danger line. Brute strength might rule such men for a time, but it took more than that to last as long as Schuster had. A brilliant mind, unscrupulous nature, complete disregard for human life and some considerable courage enabled Kale Schuster to dominate the law-breaking scene. Let Butch Cassidy, the murderous Harvey Logan, Ben Kilpatrick and other Wild Bunch leaders make newspaper headlines, behind them—making more money than all of them put together and for much less risk—was Kale Schuster. Small wonder that Zimmerman treated the man with such respect.

"About that telegraph message you sent me—" Schuster began, taking the offered seat, drink and cigar.

"I—I didn't know how else to put it," Zimmerman gasped.

"You did it real well," Schuster informed him and sipped at the drink. "How did it happen?"

Feeling relief at knowing he earned Schuster's approbation, Zimmerman went through the details of the previous night's happenings from Skerrit's arrival to sending the two long-riders after Scobie Dale's wagon. With less eagerness, he explained that the men had not yet returned.

"Maybe they didn't have a chance to catch up or something," Schuster said mildly. "Were they reliable?"

"The best I could get," answered Zimmerman evasively.

"Which could mean anything," purred Schuster, losing some of the mildness. "Do *you* think Dale took the girl to Desborough with him?"

"Everything pointed to her being with him just afore he shot Skerrit."

"Has the town been searched?"

"I've had my men asking around."

"What's the marshal here like?"

"He's safe. Do you want to see him?"

"Sure. He can go along with my men to make the search look legal. If she's still in town, I want her finding."

"What did she do?" asked Zimmerman before he could stop himself.

A bleak, unpleasant smile came to Schuster's face as he looked at his host. "Now you *don't* really want an answer to *that*, do you, Mr. Zimmerman?"

Suddenly Zimmerman found himself completely disinterested in the reason for his guest wanting Pauline's death. Rising to his feet, he told Schuster he would send for the marshal and went to do so.

Night had fallen and a thorough search of the town failed to produce Pauline. In the Liberty Bell, Schuster, Kid Tonopah and Jack Sage sat around the absent owner's desk and Joey Stinks squat on his haunches in the corner of the room.

"She's left town, that's for sure," Schuster announced. "I thought that those long-riders hadn't come back because they learned she wasn't with Dale."

"Want for me to go fetch her back?" asked Tonopah.

"No. We'll wait until the rest of the men catch up with us first," Schuster answered. "Say though, Dale's headed for Desborough."

"So?" grunted the young killer, having drunk just enough to be truculent.

"Marshal Tex Rudbeck runs the law there."

"No one-hoss town's tin-star worries me," Tonopah declared.

"Well he does me," Schuster replied.

"Then you must scare awful easy," sneered Tonopah.

"I may," admitted Schuster. "But never when all I'm dealing with is a cheap half-drunk yahoo with a gun where his brains should be."

"Meaning?" Tonopah asked.

"You figure it out—or ask a *man* to do it for you."

Tonopah's lips drew back in a snarl and he started to thrust away his chair ready to come to his feet. Half-drunk, his normally mean temper tended to be real touchy and he disliked taking orders from a short-grown dude. Half out of the chair, he froze and stared in amazement into the barrel of Schuster's revolver. Yet the other had not moved from his seat. Tonopah suddenly realized that Schuster's cross-draw rig possessed a big advantage over the buscadero gunbelt which pointed its gun butt to the rear and hung low on the thigh; it allowed the weapon to be drawn with equal ease and speed even when seated.

Then, with a sudden shock, Tonopah saw that the Colt's hammer crept back as Schuster's finger depressed the trigger. Moving another fraction of an inch, the hammer would reach its farthest rearward point and then snap forward again to drive the striker against the primer and fire the powder charge. While Schuster's Lightning might be only .38 in calibre, it looked a whole lot bigger to Tonopah at that moment.

"Easy, boss!" Sage said quietly, but earnestly. "He's only a fool kid."

For what seemed like several minutes to Tonopah, Schuster gave no sign of having heard the words. During that time the young killer looked death in the face and found the sensation unpleasant. He read Schuster's desire to complete the depression of the trigger and fought down an inclination to plead for mercy. At last the finger relaxed and the hammer sank slowly down once more to rest harmlessly in the pre-cocking position. Then, with the same flickering speed that it appeared, the gun went back into leather.

"Like I was saying," Schuster remarked as if a man's life had not hung in the balance for some thirty seconds. "Not every problem can be solved with a bullet. Rudbeck's honest and very popular in his town. You could kill the marshal here and nobody would give a damn. Cut down a popular man like Rudbeck and the scream will go up so loud that the Governor will hear it."

"I thought we'd protection up there," Sage put in.

"We have—to a certain extent," agreed Schuster. "Only one thing every politician learns is when to sing low and keep quiet. Until that girl's dead is one of those times."

Up until that moment none of the party but Schuster had any idea of why they hunted for Pauline Pitt. Even with the little he had just heard, Sage had no idea what brought about the interest in an obscure little saloon-girl. He also did not intend to press for further information.

"What'll we do then, boss?" Sage asked.

"Follow Dale to Desborough."

"And take him on the trail?"

"I think not. Sure we might be able to lay for him, but he has those dogs with him and it won't be easy to pick a place where they can't locate us first. But if he gets to Desborough without trouble, he might just start to think he's got everybody fooled and get over-confident. Over-confidence can get a man killed."

While saying the last words, Schuster looked mockingly at Kid Tonopah, but the young killer chose to ignore the hint. Instead he said, "It's only one man and a gal. Why not send Joey Stinks here after them. He could sneak up—"

"And get killed before he came within fifty yards," interrupted Schuster. "I can smell him from here. Those dogs would do it before he came within fifty yards even if the wind blew towards him. No, I reckon we'll do things my way."

"What way'll that be," asked Tonopah, then he altered his truculent tone and added, "boss?"

"Right now I wouldn't know," Schuster admitted. "I don't make long-distance plans. So we'll wait for the rest of the men to catch up with us, then follow on Dale's tracks. If the girl's with him, Joey Stinks ought to be able to find some sign of her. After that we can decide what to do."

Sitting up on the bed of a room at the Witch Creek relay station, Flax Fannon peered disbelievingly at the night-blackened window. Apparently the effects of the blow had taken more shaking off than he expected, for he slept deeply instead of merely napping for a short time. However, he felt much improved and left the room to walk downstairs.

"That you, Flax?" Caffery called from the telegraph room.

"Sure."

"Come on in."

On entering the room, Flax found the agent seated at the desk with a sheet of paper and the cipher-disk before him.

"Is that from Waco?" Flax asked.

"Sure is. How do you feel?"

"Better. What's Waco say?"

"Try reading it," Caffery grunted and offered the sheet of paper.

"Flax," the young man read. "Am headed for Desborough. Meet me there. Waco."

"I'll do just that," Flax said.

"Hope you've got a good slicker along," Caffery remarked as he locked away the cipher-disk and then burned the message. "Cause it's going to rain and hard."

"Good," grinned Flax. "That'll make the grass grow, the flowers bloom and the rivers run. It'll also wash out Scobie's trail and make sure that nobody who hasn't been there already finds out what happened in that clearing."

"I'll get you a meal afore you leave," Caffery said. "What do you aim to go and do first?"

"Head into Braddock and see if that gal and her bunch are there."

"And if they are?"

"I've not made up my mind on that yet," Flax answered. "But most likely I'll just leave them until after I've met up with Waco." He grinned. "Anyways, I don't reckon I'll find them there. Don't ask me why, but I think they've gone to Desborough."

"Must be an interesting place," said Caffery dryly, "the number of folks headed for it."

Which, considering the old agent did not know of Schuster's presence in Braddock and interest in Desborough, was a mighty shrewd observation.

CHAPTER TWELVE

News of the Killer Bear

"Has it stopped raining?" asked Pauline, stirring restlessly in the bed and looking up at Scobie Dale.

"Sure has, Pauline gal," he replied, seated on the edge of the bed and buttoning up his shirt. "We'll be in Desborough by sundown at the latest."

Looking at Scobie, the girl felt she must give a warning. The coming of the rains had brought about a change in their arrangements for sleeping accommodation. Throughout the day Scobie had intended to observe the proprieties and sleep under the wagon. When it became obvious that more than a gentle shower was coming, the girl insisted that he join her inside the Rocker ambulance's waterproof canopy.

"Nothing's changed, Scobie," she told him determinedly. "I still won't be tangled up with a hound dog man."

"Like I said before, gal," Scobie answered, coming to his feet and taking up his gunbelt, "it's your life and choice."

"There's nothing wrong with you—" she hastened to assure him.

"Except that I'm a foot-loose hound dog man," he finished for her. "Trouble being, gal, that I'll never change."

"I know," Pauline admitted. "And that's why I won't—"

"It's time we got moving," Scobie drawled.

After strapping on his gunbelt, he lifted the covers and swung on to the wagon box. With the rains ended, everything looked clean, bright and pleasant. The hound pack moved around in the early morning sun, shaking themselves and looking none the worse for a night of rain spent under the wagon. Behind Scobie, the girl swung her legs out of the bed and reached for her clothes. Just as Scobie prepared to jump from the wagon, a thought struck him.

"Stop inside," he told the girl.

"What is it?" she answered, ignoring her naked condition and taking up the carbine from where it lay alongside his Lightning rifle on the firearms chest.

"Just had me an idea, gal."

"Is *that* all?" Pauline snorted.

"Don't often get one, so it come as a surprise," smiled Scobie. "The rains have wiped out all your sign back there at the clearing. I'll swear that nobody come close enough to us yesterday to know you're along. Let's keep it that way, shall we?"

"I'll say one thing, Scobie," the girl said, putting down the rifle. "When you have an idea, it's a right smart one."

"Get dressed," he told her, "or I'll be getting another idea right now—and we don't have time for *that* right now."

Laughing, Pauline obeyed his order. Scobie dropped from the wagon and stood for a time searching the surrounding country for any sign of watching men, but he saw nothing to give a hint that anybody spied on the wagon. Collecting wood from the possum belly, he made a fire and cooked breakfast.

"I never had it so good," Pauline smiled as he passed

her plate and a cup of coffee into the wagon. "What'll we do now, Scobie?"

"Go on to Desborough, then hunt down that bear. It's got to be done."

"I know that."

"Won't be easy though, the rain's washed out more than just your tracks by this time, gal."

"How'll you do it then?" she asked.

"Wait for word of the next place that old bear kills at."

"But that might not be for days, or not even in the State."

"Nope," Scobie replied. "A grizzly bear takes him a piece of country, stakes a claim to it by making bear-trees to warn off other bears. It'll be between five and ten miles square and he'll not roam far out of it."

"He still might not kill another man," Pauline objected.

"Man or cow, gal, it's likely to be one or another of 'em. A grizzly needs meat to keep it going. Only it's not able to hunt like a cougar or a pack of buffalo wolves. So when it learns how easy it can kill cattle, it keeps on doing just that. That bear's going to kill again and soon. Happen somebody finds the kill and don't disturb the bear, I'll get word, go there and hunt it down."

"How about me?" asked the girl.

"You're coming along with me, at least until Waco comes for you."

"How about while you're in Desborough?"

"You'll just have to stay hid in the back. Nobody'll put their face inside to look. I'll see to that, and as soon as I can, we'll move away from town."

"You can't take Vixen bouncing across country far," Pauline warned.

"Nope. I'll leave her and the pups with Abe Reiger at the general store," Scobie replied. "Him and his missus're friends of mine."

"Pass me the food for Vixen when you've finished eating," the girl said. "I'd best mix it. I never yet saw a man who could make up a meal for a bitch after she welped."

"Yes, ma'am," grinned Scobie. "That old Belle's due to come into use soon. Happen she gets caught, there'll be another litter come along."

Which was the nearest he had come so far to making an offer, Pauline concluded. She ducked in a deep breath and set her lips grimly, refusing to comment one way or the other but steeling herself to refuse as gently as possible if he took the matter further. However, he did not and so she finished her breakfast, fixed up Vixen's meal and tidied the inside of the wagon while Scobie made ready to leave.

Soon after noon, Schuster and a party of men approached the site of Scobie's previous night's camp. Halting the others, Schuster ordered Joey Stinks forward to read sign. With the rain of the previous night, a perfect opportunity to learn of Pauline Pitt's presence presented itself and Schuster did not intend to miss it.

A further six men had joined him in Braddock and one of them slowed down the pace of the pursuit. Jervis Thorpe was not a skilled horseman and unused to making long, fast rides over rough hill trails. However, Schuster felt that having the politician along out-balanced the other slowing down the party.

Tall, slim, with a gaunt hook-nosed face, Thorpe looked miserable. Like most of his kind, he felt himself above the ordinary run of people and hated to be in their presence except when making a speech to build up his popularity. Thorpe possessed the rare quality of being able to keep the poorer folks believing he thought only of their welfare, yet persuade the small businessmen and others of that class to give him their backing. However, he knew that he would still be an obscure tub-thumper back East if it had not been

for Schuster. So he could not refuse when the other insisted
he came along after the girl.

Although he doubted if Thorpe would be of any use,
Schuster demanded his presence. The whole trouble came
about through the politician's stupidity and Schuster felt it
proper that Thorpe took his share in putting things right.
Much money came Thorpe's way for his production of information of use to criminals; and with little danger or risk
of detection as long as he used his head. Unfortunately, his
ideas of doing so did not show good sense. The head teller
of the Cattlemen's Trust found certain significance in deposits of large sums of money made by Thorpe. Observing
that the deposits always followed on the heels of a big
hold-up or robbery, the teller arranged a private meeting
with Thorpe. If the politician had kept his head, the whole
affair could have been handled simply and easily. Instead
of confiding with Schuster, Thorpe went to the meeting
sure that his superior brilliance and charm would smooth
things out.

Things did not smooth out. With increasing fury,
Thorpe learned that the teller demanded a fair sum of
money as a price for his silence. Not knowing that a witness watched, Thorpe slid free the blade of the sword-stick
he carried and plunged it into the offending teller's back.
Having done so, he returned to his home and told Schuster;
leaving the clearing up his stupidity made necessary to the
other man. Schuster wasted no time in futile recrimina-
tions, but hurried to the scene of the killing. On the way an
idea formed, to be put into operation. Using the teller's
keys, he opened bank and safe. By taking a large sum of
money and negotiable bonds, Schuster gave the impression
that the teller had been murdered for his keys. While
checking that nothing remained on the scene of the murder
to lead the law to Thorpe, Schuster found Pauline's vanity
bag. The girl's flight told him that she must have seen the

killing and he started to search for her. If she told her story in the right quarter, it would cause an investigation. Never under-estimating the enemy, Schuster knew others could learn what the teller discovered and so he did not mean to allow any hint to slip out.

On learning of Pauline's arrival in Braddock, Schuster sent along his most reliable man and, when Skerrit failed, took up the business himself. However, he decided the time had come when Thorpe became fully incriminated in the business which made them both rich. So Schuster demanded that Thorpe accompanied him on the hunt and killing of the girl. Thorpe was too terrified of his "employee" to refuse and rode with the main body on the trail of the faster-travelling advance party.

After making a thorough examination of the camp-site, Joey Stinks returned and looked up at Schuster.

"Feller and dogs here," he said.

"And the girl?" Thorpe asked.

"Not see-um any sign. If her here, she not leave-um tracks."

"Then she's not with Dale after all," Thorpe sniffed.

"Or he wants it to look that way," Schuster replied. "Scobie Dale's no fool. At least there's no sense in assuming he is."

"How do you mean?" Thorpe inquired.

"Dale's a hunter, can read tracks," Schuster explained patiently. "So he'd know the ground would show them to anybody following. He may still have the girl with him."

"So what do we do?"

"We go down to Easter Corner."

"Easter Corner?" Kid Tonopah put in. "Dale's not headed there."

"He will be," Schuster stated firmly. "Let's see some movement out of these horses. We've a lot of miles to cover."

Despite having the rear covers drawn down and fastened, Pauline managed to make enough of a gap in the middle for her to watch their back trail. While travelling, she made frequent studies of the rear, but saw no sign of anyone following them.

While Schuster's party had already turned off towards Easter Corner, Norah Loxton and her three men followed a trail some three miles to the north and which met the one on which Scobie's wagon rolled a short way from Desborough. In addition Norah's group made poor time due to the storm. After spending a miserable night in a small line shack, the young woman and her trio of male companions pushed on at as good a pace as they could manage towards Desborough. Nor did the trail over which they travelled offer much opportunity to move at an equivalent speed to the hound dog man's wagon.

Night had fallen when Scobie Dale brought his wagon to a halt behind the Desborough livery barn.

"Mind you stay in back and out of sight, gal," he ordered. "Have you got the carbine handy?"

"Sure," the girl answered. "What're you going to do?"

"Act just like I would if I was alone."

"That you, Scobie?" called a voice from the barn.

"Why sure. Come on out and lend a hand with my team."

"You keep them fool dogs back first, I don't want my leg chewing off."

The livery barn's owner walked forward, keeping a wary eye on Scobie's pack and grinning a welcome. Clearly he had no idea that the girl hid in the wagon and Pauline sat silent in the darkness.

"Any more bear trouble?" Scobie asked.

"Not since it killed Copson," the owner answered. "But you know how folks are when a grizzly takes to man-eating."

"Get a mite jumpy," Scobie admitted. "Where's Tex Rudbeck?"

"Down to the saloon. You can leave your pack in the shack there. I'll help you unhitch the horses, but you handle them mean hound dogs without me."

Working quickly, the two men unhitched and tended to the horses, leading all three to stalls within the building. During the journey Pauline had made up feeds for the dogs and all Scobie needed to do was collect the bowls. Luckily the barn's owner did not wonder at how Scobie managed to make up the feeds while also driving the wagon.

With the dogs fed and all but Strike housed in the shack, Scobie returned to the wagon.

"I'll bring some food and coffee back for you," he said. "Stay put and keep inside no matter what happens."

"Vixen'll look after me," smiled the girl. "And I'll catch up on some of the sleep I missed last night."

"Yeah," Scobie answered with a grin. "You do just that."

Leaving the girl safely hidden inside the Rocker ambulance, Scobie made his way towards the saloon. As usual Strike walked at the hound dog man's side, for Scobie knew he could rely on the rottweiler to behave. On reaching the saloon, he stopped outside and looked over the batwing dogs before entering. Much the usual kind of crowd greeted his eyes; townsmen, cowhands from the area, a couple of men who might be drummers; but nobody bearing the mark of the hired killer. Before the bar, tall, whang-leather tough, Marshall Tex Rudbeck stood among a bunch of his cronies and indulged in one of his favourite pastimes.

"And this's the truth, boys," declared the marshal so solemnly that everybody who knew him waited expectantly. "I had me this dog back home to Texas. Smartest critter I ever had. I tell you, if I took out a shotgun, that

dog'd scare up quail like he was some fancy Eastern set-
ting-hound. Happen I took out my old carbine, he'd go
find me a nice, fat young whitetail deer. Should I tote
along my Sharps, he'd hunt buffalo and nothing else.
When I strapped on my gunbelt and gathered a posse, that
old dog'd follow a man's tracks like he was a bloodhound.
He got that smart he started taking airs and I fixed to stop
him."

"How'd you do it, Tex?" asked Reese, always a member
of the marshal's party whether invited or not.

"Left all the guns in the house and took out my fishing
pole."

"What happened, Tex?" asked the bartender.

"Dog-my-cats if that old dog didn't start digging up
worms for bait."

A yell of laughter rose from the small group, then they
saw Scobie coming in through the doors.

"Hey, Scobie," called Reiger, the storekeeper. "Did you
ever have a dog that smart?"

"Can't rightly say I did," Scobie answered. "Had one as
stubborn as Tex's critter was smart though."

"How was that?" Reese inquired.

"I've never seen a dog like him," Scobie told the men
soberly. "That dog just wouldn't hunt a little cougar. Fact
being, he would only hunt one when he found it bigger
than the last he chased."

"What happened to him, Scobie?" asked the bartender,
knowing his place in the affair was to feed the punch-lines
to whoever told the story.

"I took him with me when I went after a cougar on that
English duke's ranch up the Little Powder. The duke's
done some hunting and got him a whole slew of fancy
trophies around the house. Well, sir, on the floor of his
living-room, he's got the hide of a real, genuine African
lion. It spreads near on across the room. That old hound

comes up and looks it over for a spell. I could see him
getting more dejected all the time and he looked kinda low
as he walks out of the room. I've never seen him since."

"Why not?" Reese wanted to know.

"Like I told you, that hound always wanted to hunt a
bigger cougar than his last," Scobie answered, poker-
faced. "So I reckon he's off looking for one that's bigger'n
than lion skin."

Again the men laughed and Scobie joined them at the
bar, Strike lying at his feet and watching the surrounding
men with alert eyes.

"You fixing to hunt down that grizzly, Scobie?" asked
Reese.

"That's what I come for," Scobie answered. "What happened, Tex?"

"The bear come down from the high country and killed
a cow. Old Wilkie found the carcass and come in for help.
Only afore he could get it, Copson, you mind him—?"

"The butcher?"

"That's him. He took after the bear with Reese's red-
bone and his Vic dog."

"Saw that dog a few times," Scobie drawled. "One of
them English pit bull-terriers. Copson wanted me to match
Strike there again' it in a fight."

"That'd've been worth seeing," put in Reese, loyal to
the memory of his departed acquaintance but also wishing
to ingratiate himself with the hound dog man.

"Would it?" growled Scobie. "I've only seen one pit dog
fight, don't reckon much on it as a sport. Know some
fellers who do a lot of it though, and one thing they always
told me was that a man who knows sic 'em about fighting
dogs won't match them as much as a pound different in
weight."

"They didn't come any gamer than old Vic," objected
Reese. "Why I bet he went straight in at that bear—"

"And died afore he reached it," interrupted Scobie. "Which same, Strike here's run down between ten and fifteen grizzlies and he's still alive."

"There was a telegraph message came in for you this afternoon, Scobie," the marshal put in before any other discussion could develop. Taking a buff-coloured sheet of paper from his pocket, he offered it to the hound dog man. "Paxton at the depot figured you'd come to see me first off."

Taking the paper, Scobie opened it and read it. Before he could make any comments on the contents, he saw the Wells Fargo depot agent enter the saloon. Crossing to where Scobie stood, the agent held out an identical sheet of paper.

"This just come in, Scobie, and I reckon Tex might as well keep it for you. You're getting mighty popular."

"I always knowed I would," Scobie replied and read the second message. "Feller up Easter Corner way got chased by a grizzly this morning. Could be the same one as killed Copson. I'd best go over and look around. Say, Abe, can I leave my Vixen bitch with you? She just whelped and I don't want her disturbing."

"Feel free, as long as I get to buy a pup from you," Reiger replied.

"You can take second pick," promised Scobie. "I want to keep a dog and bitch pup and you can take what you want from the rest."

"Fetch her round when you feel like it," Reiger offered.

"Thanks," Scobie said. "I'll grab a meal now and then catch some sleep. I want to start for Easter Corner at dawn."

On reaching the wagon, Scobie climbed in, lowered the covering at the front and lit the lamp. Pauline stirred on the bed, looking up and reaching for the carbine. Then she relaxed and smiled up at Scobie.

"I had a meal," she told him. "Some pemmican and honey."

"Got you something hot and a can of coffee here," he replied. "Get up and pour it out, gal."

"You're beginning to sound like a husband as well as act like one," Pauline sniffed, but rose to obey.

"I got two messages," Scobie told her after they had fed. "One telling me that bear's been seen up Easter Corner way. This's the other."

Pauline read, *"Dale, Desborough. Hope to catch that one-eyed tom cougar, but will join you and inspect bitch pup first. D. Smith. Two Forks, Utah."*

"But—" she began.

"It's from Waco. When he first hit Two Forks he didn't want his name known and folks started calling him Drifter Smith.* While I was on his place, we ran down a tom cougar that'd been living high off the hog on BM beef, it only had one eye. You can bet Waco sent this to me."

Even though he spoke casually, Scobie could not help but admire the way in which Waco sent word of his intentions and made sure of giving proof of his identity. Few outsiders, if any, would understand the reference to the one-eyed tom cougar or even know of the incident involving it.

"What do we do next then?" asked the girl. "Are we waiting here for him?"

"Nope. I have to hunt that bear and folks'd start to think happen I stayed here instead of going after it. Maybe I could ask the Reigers to let you—"

"No!" the girl snapped. "I'd rather take my chances and run. Anybody who helps me's in trouble, Scobie."

"You're right, gal," agreed Scobie. "Comes morning we'll take the wagon and head for Easter Corner."

*Told in *The Drifter*.

CHAPTER THIRTEEN

The Sign of the Bear Tree

Although Schuster placed men about half-way between Desborough and Easter Corner, they learned nothing. Instead of following the winding trail, Scobie took a more direct route overland. Sure that nobody would be around to observe them, he allowed the girl to sit on the box with him.

"That's a bear-tree, isn't it?" Pauline asked, pointing to a lodgepole pine which they approached.

"It sure is," Scobie agreed and halted the wagon. "Let's take a look at it."

Ordering the pack to stay back, Scobie jumped from the wagon and helped the girl down. Together they walked towards the tree and examined its scarred trunk. A slight frown came to Scobie's face as he noticed the height of the scratches and then bent down to take and study one of the torn-out chips of wood.

"I wonder why a bear does it," Pauline said. "Back home in Kentucky we get trees just like this."

"Sure," Scobie agreed. "*Just* like it." He dropped the chip and looked around him with interest. "Reckon you dare stay out here alone for a spell?"

"While you go after the bear?" she asked.

"While I go on into Easter Corner."

"I—I reckon I might," Pauline said, sounding just a mite dubious. "When did the bear do this?"

"Two, maybe three hours back."

"And you want me to stay out here?"

"Not close to this tree. We'll move on a piece until we find a better place for you and I'll leave Whip with you while I'm gone."

"That grizzly's killed and ate one man, hasn't it?" Pauline said as they returned to the wagon.

"So they tell me," admitted Scobie.

"You think I'll be safe out here?"

"I reckon you will."

"I'll do it then—but I'm damned if I know why."

"You'd best keep the carbine," Scobie told her. "Just in case."

"*That'll* be a lot of use," sniffed the girl.

"It stopped a two-hundred-and-thirty-pound cougar," Scobie reminded her. "And happen that grizzly should show, climb a tree, poke the gun down and hit him right between his two eyes."

"Bears can climb," Pauline stated.

"Black and cinnamon bears can, maybe a young grizzly will, but not a big full-grown pappy. If you get up a tree, you'll be safe."

"That's nice to know," said Pauline, still sounding dubious.

"I want you to clear everything you own out of the wagon, and keep it with you, gal," Scobie went on. "Do it as soon as we start moving. I don't want a single thing to show that you've been with me."

"Scared I'll ruin your good name?" she smiled.

"You might say that," grinned Scobie and swung the girl on to the box. Mounting himself, he started the team moving and bellowed at the pack as they showed interest in the tree. Then, while the girl gathered her belongings, he gave her instructions, "I'll be back by nightfall if I can, but take blankets and some food in case I'm not. Let it get good and dark before you make a fire, don't make it a big one; and, happen I'm not back by dawn, put the fire out before it gets light. Smoke rising in the morning's given away more hidden men than were ever found by their fire's light in the night."

Still looking puzzled, the girl nodded and continued her packing. Quickly she gathered all her property, searching to make sure she left nothing behind, laid in a supply of food and a couple of blankets, then checked the carbine's loads. With everything prepared, she turned to ask Scobie the meaning of his orders.

"Here'll do just fine, gal," he said before she could utter a word.

On the face of it, Scobie's choice did not have the makings of a good camp-site. Pauline looked at a barren cluster of rocks, without even a few bushes close by; although a solitary Engelmann spruce tree reared stubbornly up not far from the rocks.

"Reckon you could climb it?" Scobie asked, indicating the tree.

"If I have to," Pauline replied, studying the area without favour. "Do you want me to stay here?"

Taking Pauline's face between his big hands, Scobie kissed her gently on the lips, and then looked down at her.

"Do you trust me, gal?"

"I trust you," she breathed.

"Believe me, this's the best place for you to stay until I come back. Whip'll look out for you and let you know if anything, or anybody, comes around. I'd like to leave Strike as well, but folks'd miss him and start asking questions."

"If leaving Whip'll make you short-handed, you'd best take him along," Pauline offered.

"I reckon I can handle things without him," Scobie replied.

During the time she accompanied Scobie, Pauline gained the confidence of his pack and they accepted her as they had no other person. Despite their first meeting, Whip, the big young Plott, took a special fancy to the girl and followed her around in a protective manner. Not that Pauline spoiled any of the dogs, even Whip. When they behaved, she praised them but should one of the pack disobey her, she corrected it straight away.

Although Scobie tied a length of rope around Whip's neck, the Plott caused no fuss at being left with the girl. Knowing Scobie wanted to be moving, Pauline asked no questions. She collected her property, gathered wood from the possum belly, some food and filled the coffee-pot from the wagon's keg. Taking her load, the carbine and hound to a sheltered spot among the rocks, she watched Scobie drive the wagon away.

"Damned if I know what this's about, Whip," she said. "But I reckon Scobie knows best. Let's hope he's back before dark."

Holding his team and wagon to a steady pace, Scobie continued to Easter Corner. Although originally built as a relay station by the ubiquitous Wells Fargo Company, Easter Corner blossomed into a thriving hamlet of twenty houses—provided one counted the station buildings and saloon. That even twenty houses be required for the population might have surprised some people, but Scobie knew that Easter Corner did not merely rely upon a twice-weekly stage for its livelihood. Cattle herds watered nearby when making the trip to the Laramie railroad. Members of the Wild Bunch long-riding on the Outlaw Trail found Easter Corner a convenient spot in which to rest tired horses. In fact the saloon's fittings and equipment often surprised people who did not know the hamlet's true purpose, being far more luxuriant than one might expect.

With this knowledge of Easter Corner as an outlaw hangout, Scobie had not felt happy about taking Pauline there in the first place. Once he read and understood the message of the bear-tree, he knew that he must leave her behind. Studying several saddle-horses in the visitors' corral behind the station, he guessed that the precaution would be justified.

A man rose from the seat on the saloon's porch as Scobie's wagon entered town, walked to the batwing doors and spoke to somebody inside. Clearly he announced Scobie's arrival for three men left the saloon and walked towards the wagon. Bringing the wagon to a halt, Scobie swung down without giving any hint of being aware of the approaching trio's interest in him. Yet he studied them and knew he called the play correctly. Although Schuster had not been with Thorpe on the Governor's cougar hunt, Scobie recognized him as well as identifying the politician. He did not know Kid Tonopah's name, but could tell *what* the other was. Even before the men came close, Scobie knew Tonopah had drunk enough bottled bravemaker to make him dangerously truculent and proddy.

"Settle down, boys," Scobie told the pack and they flopped around the wagon.

"Hello there, Mr. Dale," Thorpe greeted in his best "Vote-for-me-and-a-square-deal" voice.

"Howdy, Mr. Thorpe," Scobie replied, lifting the Lightning rifle from the wagon box. "You're a mite off your home range."

"You might say that," agreed Thorpe. "This is Scobie Dale, Mr. Schuster. I told you about that cougar hunt he took me on. Lord, I can still feel the bruises."

Schuster directed a glance at the front of the wagon, but could not see into it due to the covers hanging closed.

Turning his eyes towards Scobie, he studied the scarred face. The big hound dog man seemed quite at ease and unconcerned by finding Pauline's enemies in Easter Corner.

"Mr. Thorpe told me about how you've got that Rocker ambulance fitted up," Schuster said. "A regular home on wheels. Mind if I take a look inside at it?"

"One of my bitches dropped a litter and I've been carrying her in the wagon—" Scobie replied, meaning to go on after seeing how his apparent refusal affected the others.

Moving in front of Schuster and Thorpe, Kid Tonopah thrust his face forward and prepared to show them how to deal with such a situation.

"The boss said he wants to look in that wagon," he stated. "And it'll take more than a ragged pants hound do—"

All the time he spoke, Tonopah watched Scobie's rifle-filled right hand. If the other took exception to the words, he ought to either let the rifle fall and reach for that single-shooting Remington pistol, or make his play with the Lightning. In either case, Tonopah figured the movement would give him due warning.

Only Scobie did not act in the required manner. An instant too late, Tonopah saw Scobie's left fist bunch and drive upwards. Gliding in a pace, Scobie threw a beautiful punch which connected under Tonopah's jaw with all the hound dog man's weight behind it. Tonopah's head snapped rearwards. He jerked up on to his toes, then went over to crash on his back in the centre of the street. Even without giving the sprawled-out young killer another glance, Scobie knew there would be no trouble from that source for some time to come.

Sage, the man who had been on the porch, gave an angry growl, started to move forward and reached for his gun. From stretching Tonopah unconscious on the ground,

Scobie's left hand circled and caught the foregrip of the Lightning as his right hand swung it upwards. Before he could complete the move, Scobie saw Schuster swing angrily towards the advancing man.

"Cut it out, Sage!" Schuster barked. "The Kid got what he asked for."

"Which same's the best advice you've ever had, mister," Scobie went on and nodded towards the wagon.

Following the direction of Scobie's gaze, Sage saw that the rottweiler had come to its feet and now stood on stiff legs, its back hair up and teeth showing in a menacing snarl.

"See what you mean," Sage remarked, standing very still.

"Get this damned fool on his feet and away from here," Schuster ordered, then turned his attention to Scobie once more. "I'm sorry about that, Mr. Dale. You know what these fool kids are."

"I reckon I do," agreed Scobie and lowered the rifle.

"If you don't want us to look in your wagon—"

"Shucks, that jasper didn't let me finish. I was going to say that my Vixen bitch whelped down in it, but I left her in Desborough. Come ahead and take a look inside."

Throwing a searching glance at Scobie, Schuster advanced and climbed on to the wagon box. He drew up the covers and peered inside, then climbed into the vehicle. Without a glance in Schuster's direction, Scobie looked at the nervous face of Thorpe.

"Where-at's this feller as almost got ate by the bear, Mr. Thorpe?"

"Hugh?" grunted the politician.

"'Course, you likely wouldn't know. I got word there's a man-hunting grizzly up this way."

"We've only just arrived," Thorpe said, darting nervous glances from Scobie to the wagon.

Relief showed on Thorpe's face as Schuster appeared at the front of the wagon. Jumping down, the man walked over to Scobie.

"Mighty comfortable," he said.

"Hey, Scobie!" called a voice and the Wells Fargo agent came trotting up with a telegraph message form in his hand. The man darted a calculating glance at Schuster as he handed over the paper. "This just come in from Desborough for you."

Accepting the form, Scobie read its message and slowly raised his eyes to look over the men before him. "Who was it got chased by that grizzly here?"

"Hell, that was my roustabout," the agent answered, again glancing at Schuster and clearly signalling a message. "Only I don't reckon it was a grizzly at all right now."

"How do you mean?" asked Schuster, just a hint of warning and menace in his voice.

"This message from Desborough says the grizzly's killed a cow and a prize bull up there," explained the agent.

"That's what it says," Scobie agreed. "Where-at's this roustabout?"

"Sleeping off a whisky-jag right now," the agent answered. "Hell, Scobie, I didn't even know he'd sent that message until this morning."

"That's too bad!" snorted Thorpe, feeling called upon to make a contribution to the conversation. "Mr. Dale is a busy man and shouldn't have his time wasted on wild-goose chases."

"Feller like me gets used to that," Scobie drawled. "I'd best be getting back to Desborough."

"Won't you stay here for a meal at least, Mr. Dale?" asked Schuster. "I think that Wells Fargo owes you something for your trouble."

"They pay me regular to hunt their stock-killers," replied Scobie. "That grizzly's got to be stopped, too. But I'll rest my hosses and have a meal."

Over the meal Schuster sought for some hint that Scobie knew of Pauline and came to the conclusion finally that he did not. While discussing the trouble with Skerrit, Scobie declared himself unable to think why he butted in and commented that the calico-cat who started all the fuss did not even stick around to thank him for his help. The meal over, Scobie stated his intention to start back for Desborough. He used his run-in with Kid Tonopah as an added reason for going, although the young man had been taken to the hamlet's doctor — long-rider trade made it possible for a medical man to make his living in Easter Corner — who now worked to weld together the broken jaw bones.

"He'll not forget that I bust it for him," Scobie stated. "So I'll head out now and save fuss."

"She's not with him after all," Thorpe declared as he stood with Schuster and watched the wagon leave town.

"I'm just about ready to believe it," Schuster replied. "There wasn't a thing in the wagon to show that she'd been there."

"He'd've brought her with him, even if he kept her hidden," insisted Thorpe. "He couldn't have known we were waiting here."

"There's no way he could," Schuster agreed. "That was quick thinking on the agent's part, the way he handled the message from Desborough. I'll see he gets paid for it."

Although Schuster went along with his employer in hating to think any man could out-smart him, he was prepared to admit that it might be done. However, after balancing up the situation, he concluded that it would be in keeping with Pauline's ways to lay a false scent; just as she did by getting a friend to take a stage East in her place. Knowing Scobie's popularity with certain high-up members of the

Wild Bunch, Schuster felt relieved to know he would not need to order the hound dog man's death.

"What do we do now?" asked Thorpe.

"Go back to Cheyenne," Schuster replied and led the way into the saloon. "Only we'll go through Desborough. Dale might just be playing it tricky." He looked to where his men sat at the bar. "Where's Joey Stinks?"

"Under the table there," Sage replied. "Want for me to trail after Dale?"

"No. It'll be dark soon and only the Indian might have been able to keep close enough to Dale to do any good, without being caught at it."

"I only asked hoping you'd say 'no'," grunted Sage.

"Tell the boys we'll not be riding until morning," Schuster ordered and walked towards the bar.

When the sun went down, Scobie fastened the wagon team's reins to the brake handle and allowed the two horses to keep moving. He knew he could rely on them to continue at the same leisurely pace for a time and so freed the zebra dun. Leaving his riding horse standing with a trailing hackamore, he moved back a short way accompanied by the dogs. In the shelter of a rock, he waited until sure that nobody followed. When certain, he rose and returned to the waiting dun, mounted it and caught up to the wagon.

Pauline had just decided to make a fire when Whip rose and stared off into the darkness. Even as she reached for the carbine, the girl realized that the big Plott would not be wagging its tail in a delighted manner unless friends approached. For all that, she remained in cover until the wagon drew nearer and Scobie called to her.

"See that mean ole grizzly didn't come and eat you, gal," Scobie said as he took her belongings from her.

"I never saw it," the girl replied and climbed on to the box.

"You'd had damned good eye-sight if you had," Scobie

drawled. "It's never been on this side of Desborough."

"But we saw that bear-tree," Pauline pointed out.

"Just like you got back home in Kentucky," agreed Scobie. "That's when I knew there wasn't a grizzly hereabouts."

"I don't get you."

"You saw the height of those scratches and bites, gal. Weren't none of them over five foot high. A grizzly only that size'd be too young to kill off a full-grown whiteface cow, or to make a bear-tree. And neither black nor cinnamon* bear sticks around when a full-grown grizzly moves into the area. Or if it does, it's too smart to start throwing out challenges by making a bear-tree."

"But that message?"

"Just a pack of lies, gal, to have me bring you to Easter Corner. Schuster and a bunch of hired guns were waiting there."

"So *that's* why you left me behind!" Pauline said. "But couldn't you have picked a better place?"

"There wasn't one between here and Easter Corner," Scobie replied. "Good hiding-place, a tree you could shin up happen I called it wrong about the grizzly, and no berry-bushes or anything else to attract a bear of any kind."

"You know something, Scobie Dale," the girl said. "You're a real smart feller."

"Hell, gal," Scobie answered. "It was you who put me on to the thing in the first place."

"Me! How did I do it?"

"Mind how you said that you had trees like that back home in Kentucky?"

"Sure."

"Well you have. *Just* like it. Black and cinnamon bears make bear-trees as well as a grizzly—only there's never

The cinnamon bear is a colour phase of the black species.

been any grizzly bears east of the Big Muddy."†

"And that's how you knew the telegraph message was a lie?" Pauline asked.

"It made me so sure that I didn't fix to take you into Easter Corner," Scobie admitted. "Schuster searched the wagon, talked some to me. I reckon we might've thrown him off our line for a spell."

†*Big Muddy: The Mississippi River.*

CHAPTER FOURTEEN

Scobie's Mistake

"This time the message's true, Pauline gal," Scobie said as he allowed the girl to join him on the wagon box. "Do the shirt and pants fit you?"

"Sure," Pauline replied. "I'll keep them until I've had a chance to take a bath. Maw always used to tell us kids never to put on clean clothes unless we'd had a bath first."

It was shortly before noon on the day following Scobie's visit to Easter Corner and Scobie drove his wagon out across the rolling range country towards the scene of the grizzly bear's latest assault on a ranch's cattle. During the time Scobie spent checking on the validity of the report, Pauline remained concealed in the wagon. However, she had asked him to pick up a change of clothing and he bought a shirt and pair of levis pants for her. The size of the two items caused Mrs. Reiger to remark they would never fit him, but he made up a story which he hoped would satisfy her curiosity.

Although Scobie did not know it, interested parties watched his arrival and made note of the purchase. Scobie had not noticed Elmhurt in the Liberty Bell at Braddock and so failed to recognize the man as he made the purchase for Pauline.

Elmhurt watched Scobie leave town, then headed to the

rooming house and the waiting Norah and Wilfred Loxton.
Quickly he told what he had seen, mentioning how he and
Laverick hoped to look in the rear of the hound dog man's
wagon but failed due to Scobie's pack being around it.

"Those damned dogs don't take to strangers," Elmhurt
finished. "They looked mean enough to tear a man apart if
he went near the wagon."

"It's lucky you didn't go near then," Norah sniffed. "I
said keep clear of it. Stop trying to think for yourself.
We're too close to the girl to have it loused up now."

"Dale has the girl with him," Loxton stated.

"I'm sure of it," his sister agreed. "That's who the
clothes are for."

"When do we go after her?" Elmhurt asked.

"*We* don't," Norah replied.

"Why?"

"Because, Mr. Elmhurt, Dale wouldn't let us. The marshal here is his friend and Rudbeck wouldn't be any too
pleased when he learned who we are."

"Then what do we do?" Loxton asked.

"Nothing yet," Norah answered. "We'll give them a
couple of hours' start and then follow their tracks. I suppose you *can* do that, Mr. Elmhurt?"

"I reckon I can," Elmhurt agreed. "But why wait that
long?"

"I want them to think that nobody suspects them or is
following them," the girl explained. "When they make
camp, I'll go in alone first. I can think up a story to satisfy
Dale if he's there. If he isn't, I can handle the girl."

"It's your play," Elmhurt grunted.

"I know it. Just don't spoil things by trying to make any
smart moves like coming after me too soon."

Schuster's party arrived in Desborough shortly after
noon. Not wishing for people to know that Jervis Thorpe
associated with hired gun-hands, Schuster had the men

drift in at intervals and act as strangers. While visiting the store to buy cigars, Schuster overheard Mrs. Reiger discussing Scobie's purchase with another woman. Although accepting that the hound dog man *might* be picking up the clothing for a friend on one of the local ranches, Schuster decided to check the story out. After sending Sage, Joey Stinks and another man out with orders to follow Scobie's wagon, Schuster made rapid plans and gave certain orders to the remainder of his party, including a part for Thorpe to play.

Unaware of their danger, Scobie and Pauline rode the slow-moving wagon through the wooded lowlands and approached the more open hill country. They talked of various things while moving, happy in their belief that they had shaken off the pursuit for the time at least. Suddenly Scobie brought the wagon to a halt and started across the rolling land ahead of them.

"What is it?" the girl asked.

"Up there, going towards the top of that rim," he replied.

"I can't see anything," she told him.

"Grab my field-glasses from in the wagon," Scobie suggested.

Obeying, the girl raised and focused the powerful binoculars then raked the slope. A sensation like an icy hand touching her spine ran through the girl at what she saw. Ambling along in its hump-backed, careless way, a huge grizzly bear passed up the distant slope and out of sight over the top.

"Is it the one?" she whispered, although the bear would be almost a mile away.

"It's the one," Scobie replied. "You don't get two bears that size in one area, at least not this early in the year. After May you might find a couple, but they'd have come looking for a mate."

"What're you going to do?" asked the girl.

"Find a place to make a camp, then go after him."

"Will there be time for you to catch up to him before dark?"

"Time enough, gal. We'll be so close behind him that he won't run far. I've never yet seen a grizzly keep running when the hounds pushed him hard. He'll almost always stand and fight."

Flicking the reins, Scobie started the team moving in the direction of the rim. Before he had covered much more than a hundred yards, he found a place in which he felt the girl could safely be left. Turning the wagon down into a small hollow, Scobie brought it to a halt at the bottom.

"You can get off after the bear, if you like," the girl told him. "I'll see to things here."

"Let me help you with the horses first," Scobie replied. "One way or another we won't be going any farther tonight."

"Then I'll make up the dogs' feed while you're gone," Pauline promised.

After Scobie unhitched the team, Pauline led them aside and tethered them on good grazing. She could tell just how dangerous Scobie regarded the hunt, for, despite having given them a thorough cleaning the previous night, he checked both the Lightning rifle and the Remington pistol before saddling the zebra dun.

"Do you want to keep Whip here?" he asked.

"You'll need him," Pauline replied. "Don't argue, Scobie, I'll be all right while you're gone. Good luck."

"Thanks, gal. I'll try to fetch you back his hide for a bed-robe."

Showing considerable interest and excitement, for they knew that there would be hunting when their master left the wagon and mounted the dun stallion, the pack fanned out around Scobie as he rode up out of the hollow. While climbing the slope up which the bear passed, Scobie kept his attention on the rim above him. The grizzly could be travelling, or it might be headed for a den-hole. Either way, Scobie intended to locate it, if possible, before it saw him. On first seeing the bear, Scobie noted various land-marks to help him pick up its tracks. However, he did not need to bother.

Ranging out ahead of the rest of the pack and her mas-ter, Belle came to a sudden halt. Hot to her nostrils came the raw scent of the grizzly bear, wafted in her direction from the scent-line. Her nostrils quivered and the back hair rose up stiff along her spine. If that had been cougar, or even black bear, her tail would have wagged; instead it stood up stiff as a poker. Snuffling in the scent, she cut loose with a somewhat querulous medium bawl instead of her full, ringing bugle note.

"Lay to, Belle!" Scobie whooped encouragingly, even as the rest of the pack headed for the bluetick bitch with their heads raised and noses working to catch the scent which interested her. "Go get him, dogs!"

Forward swept the pack, their voices lifting as they ran. With so hot a scent they barely troubled to lower their heads to the ground. The pack's trail-music wafted back to Pauline, although she could see nothing of them, and she felt a quiver of anxiety. Then she gave a shrug. If Scobie Dale could not take care of himself by now, he had no right to call himself a hound dog man.

Up the slope went the pack, with Scobie following at his dun's best speed. Once over it, the dogs ran on at a speed no horse could hope to equal when carrying a saddle and rider. The line ran in a straight line; no grizzly needed to walk warily or hide from any creature once it attained its full size. Ahead lay a large clump of bushes and the pack bore down in that direction, but they did not rush blindly into the thick growth. Experience of the hardest kind taught them the ways of their prey and they sensed the danger ahead. So they hovered on the outer edge of the bushes and raised their voices in savage challenge. A roaring snort sounded from the bushes as the grizzly realized that its intended ambush had failed to bring the dogs into striking distance. Turning around, it smashed through the bushes and burst out on the opposite side to the pack.

Hearing their prey on the move, the pack charged forward, wending their way through the bushes and picking up the bear's trail on the other side. A grizzly could run fast, but not as swiftly as those superbly fit, hard-muscled dogs. Fastest of the pack, although not far ahead of the rest, Song, the treeing-Walker, saw the bear first and his running-trail chop turned to a wildly excited turkey-mouth. Seconds later the remainder of the pack announced that they too saw the quarry and now ran on vision rather than scent. Increasing their pace, they spread out ready to converge on the bear and bring it to bay.

The bear ran faster, hoping to leave its noisy pursuers behind. Crashing through clumps of bushes with no more effort than if they had been blades of grass, the bear kept its lead. Then a patch of clear, open country lay ahead. That was what the pack waited for, being too wise to voluntarily close and fight where they could not move freely. Before the grizzly reached the centre of the open land, the pack forced it to halt and fight.

Coming around in a rump-scraping turn, the grizzly lashed out with a paw but Song twisted aside. This time the bear did not face the blindly game courage of a pit bull-terrier bred to go into the attack regardless of any danger. Instead it met the coldly calculating pack tactics of trained big-game hounds. Such dogs did not rush in heedlessly against their prey. While some held the bear's attention from the front and a safe distance, others darted in to slash at its flanks, rump and rear legs. In that way they pre-

vented the grizzly from concentrating on any one of them
and stopped it running farther before their master could
come up to play his part.

Scobie knew better than ride up too close. Steady and
well-trained the dun might be, but mare never raised a foal
which would stand steady in the face of the determined
charge by a grizzly bear. Dropping from his saddle a good
fifty yards from the fight, Scobie left the dun standing with
trailing reins. Under normal conditions, the hanging reins
would serve to hold the horse just as well as if they had
been fastened to a branch or tree-trunk. However, if the
bear should happen to pass Scobie and make for the dun,
the free-hanging reins would not impede the horse's
escape.

Holding his rifle ready for use, Scobie walked forward.
The fight took place about thirty yards out in the clearing,
but Scobie did not offer to fire while still in the wooded
land. All too well he knew the tenacity with which a
grizzly bear clung to life. If he shot and did not kill, the
bear would go berserk. It might run, although more likely
to charge, and escape the hounds. The United States possessed no more dangerous creature than a grizzly bear
maddened with the pain of a wound.

So Scobie knew he must move in so close that he could
not miss even though the bear moved, jinking and weaving
its head as it slashed at the surrounding dogs. Not until he
had halved the distance to the fight did Scobie come to a
halt. He felt again the wild, primeval excitement of the
hunt; a sensation which went back to the dim days of history when men went out to battle with primitive weapons
and against creatures even larger and more dangerous than
the grizzly bear. Not that Scobie's position was any sine-
cure. Even with the ultimate of black powder fire power
instead of a spear with a fire-hardened wood, or bronze

head, a man could not be assured of victory at such a moment.

When the bear saw Scobie approaching, it appeared to realize that the man presented an even more deadly danger than the dogs. Letting out an awe-inspiring roar, and looking far larger than its great size due to its hair being erected in rage, the grizzly charged straight at Scobie. Wisely the dogs before it leapt aside instead of trying to halt its progress and those at the sides or behind fell back a little.

Throwing up his rifle, Scobie took aim at the bear's head. There would be little enough time, but he knew better than shoot wildly. Gently he squeezed the Lightning's trigger—and a dull click rewarded his efforts. Even as he started to work the "trombone" slide of the cocking mechanism, Scobie could not prevent himself from taking an involuntary pace to the rear. His foot caught against something and he tripped over backwards to fall right in the path of the charging bear. Letting out a roaring snarl, Strike flung himself forward and his powerful jaws seized hold of the bear's left rear leg. Even the rottweiler's hundred pounds of solid weight could not halt the bear's progress or even slow it to any great extent.

At such a moment a hound dog man's life hung in the balance and depended on the spirit and loyalty of his pack. With hounds cowed by harsh training methods, Scobie would have died. However, he treated his pack with firm kindness, retaining their spirits rather than crushing them under. Those dogs would willingly face any danger to protect him.

An instant after Strike gripped hold of the bear's left leg, Bugle's jaws clamped on to the right. Then Belle, Whip, Dick, Song and Tiger, the last bluetick, closed in to grab hold where they could. Tiger, blocked by the others on the flanks, went for the bear's throat and missed death by inches as its powerful jaws chopped savagely at him.

Altogether the seven dogs did not quite equal the grizzly's seven-hundred-and-fifty-pound weight, but their combined assault slowed it down.

Scobie twisted himself over in a hurried roll and the bear's mouth closed so near that he felt its breath on his shirt while the long-clawed feet landed where he lay a split second before. Unfortunately, Scobie had lost his rifle when he fell and been forced to roll away from it. He continued rolling, not wishing to impede his dogs.

Foiled in its attack on Scobie, the bear vented its rage on the dogs. However, they knew the game too well to hang on when its head or paws came their way and showed a remarkable agility in leaping clear of danger. Of course, the moment the bear tried to attack one side, the dogs on the other increased their efforts. Belle caught a long but shallow gash from a claw and Tiger's right ear ripped open in a real narrow escape when the bear's teeth grabbed it and tore through.

Coming to his feet, Scobie knew he must act, and quickly, before more serious injuries happened to his dogs. The rifle lay beyond the fighting animals and might not work even if he reached it. Which left only the big pistol; accurate, powerful, yet not the kind of weapon one would select when going up against a full-grown grizzly bear. Scobie carried the big Remington more as a last-ditch defensive weapon rather than for dispatching an uninjured bear, but beggars could not be choosers.

With the Remington in his hand, cocked and ready for use, Scobie gave rapid consideration to his next move. Darting to one side, he approached the bear from the rear. If only his pack held its attention for a short time, he might succeed in his plan.

Sucking in a breath, Scobie stepped forward. He saw the bear's head start to swing in his direction and shoved the muzzle of the Remington just below where the ear joined the skull. Even as the bear realized its danger, the gun cracked. With a bullet large enough to be fired in a rifle, the Remington packed sufficient power to drive its load through the bear's skull and into the brain beneath the wall of bone. Not even the mighty grizzly bear could withstand such a blow. Its jaws snapped convulsively as the mighty frame crumpled and it toppled to the ground. Leaping backwards as soon as he fired, Scobie started to throw open the Remington's breech while still in the air. Deftly his left hand scooped a bullet from the belt loops and fed it into the chamber as the empty case flew out.

With his Remington reloaded, he circled the dogs and quivering shape of the bear to reach his rifle. Typical of the man, Scobie checked on the cause of the misfire before attempting to approach the bear. He found the trouble to be caused by a faulty primer in the cartridge, something which could only be detected by squeezing the trigger. There could hardly have been a worse time for such a mishap. If the pack had failed to impede the bear's charge, there would be no need for Pauline to fear that she might become entangled with a foot-loose hound dog man.

"All right, you bunch," he called to the pack as they worried at the bear's motionless body. "Get out of it. Happen you spoil that hide, Pauline'll fix your wagon but g—"

The words chopped off abruptly as he heard the distant crackle of revolver then rifle shots. Having spent most of his life in the open range country, Scobie possessed an inborn sense of direction. Anxiety gnawed at him as he ran towards the waiting zebra dun, for he knew that the shooting came from where he had left the girl.

CHAPTER FIFTEEN

Miss Loxton's Profession

While listening to the sound of the hounds growing farther away, Pauline brought the feed bowls to the rear of the wagon ready for when she began preparing the dogs' food. Then she heard the sound of approaching hooves, squeak of leather and rumble of turning wheels. Reaching for the carbine, she looked up at the top of the fold. A buckboard driven by a smartly-dressed, beautiful woman came into view and started down the slope in Pauline's direction.

If there had been a man accompanying the buckboard, Pauline would have kept the carbine in her hands. Seeing only the woman, she relaxed, set the carbine back on the bed of the wagon and waited to see what brought the other girl out on the range without an escort.

A feeling of satisfaction ran through Norah Loxton as she brought the buckboard to a halt. After a long search, she had found the girl Schuster wanted to kill and who might hold the key to the big Cattlemen's Trust bank robbery. More to the point, she found Pauline Pitt alone and the diminishing sound of the hounds meant that Scobie Dale would not be returning for some time. Having made better time than Scobie, the girl's party came into sight just in time to see him ride from the hollow and head up the rim. On hearing from Laverick what that meant, Norah

ordered the men to stay put while she went in and captured
the girl. Having noticed the quick way in which the small
girl picked up the Winchester carbine, and her competent
handling of it, Norah knew she called the play right. Seeing a party of people coming, Pauline would either run or
fight; most probably fight, and the sound of shooting might
reach the hound dog man's ears.

"Howdy," Pauline greeted.

"Hello," Norah answered. "Are you alone, too."

"My man's just gone out after that stock-killing
grizzly," Pauline replied. "Light down and rest your feet.
I'll be making coffee as soon as I light a fire."

"Thank you," Norah said, swinging from the buggy and
walking towards Pauline.

Expecting to have to charm away Scobie Dale's suspi-
cions, Norah had let her hair down and left her jacket in the
rear of the buckboard. Her blouse and skirt might be deco-
rous, yet she gave them the appearance of being as reveal-
ing and eye-catching as any saloon-girl's dress.

"Are you out with friends?" Pauline inquired.

"Oh no. I'm just on my way to visit with my aunt.
Don't let me stop you working."

Pauline started to turn towards the wagon, as if meaning
to carry on with her work. However, she watched her visi-
tor out of the corner of her eye and saw Norah reach for
something concealed in the skirt's waistband.

Under normal conditions Pauline would have thought
nothing of Norah's arrival, or the movement. Pauline had
not lived normally since witnessing Thorpe commit
murder. Nor were conditions normal around Desborough.
No woman would make an unescorted journey through an
area where a grizzly bear reputed to be a man-eater
roamed. So the little blonde stayed on the alert and did not
hesitate when she saw Norah begin to draw a Remington
Double Derringer from its place of concealment.

Spinning around, Pauline flung herself forward and caught Norah's wrist before the Derringer could come into line. Jerking at the trapped wrist, Pauline pivoted as she had in childhood scuffles and rammed her buttocks against Norah's body then levered the big girl over. Norah gave a squeal of surprise as her feet left the ground. Letting the Derringer fall, she landed rump first and twisted around to see the little blonde bending to pick up her gun.

Fury filled Norah and she lunged forward, her hands reaching for the Derringer. Pauline saw that the other girl might reach it and kicked it aside. Then she jumped clear of Norah's grabbing hands. Before Pauline could decide on whether to make another try for the Derringer or dash to the wagon and the carbine, Norah rose and faced her.

Before going into her chosen profession, Norah had attended a select college for women and belonged to a rabidly feminist group. Among other things, her faction learned self-defence and indulged in boxing matches as a further proof that they could do anything men could. Having achieved some success in the ring against her friends, she expected no trouble in handling the smaller, lighter, untrained girl.

"All right!" she hissed, cocking her fists in the approved manner. "I'll—"

Unfortunately for Norah's plan, Pauline had never even seen a boxing match and knew nothing of the noble art. What the little blonde did know *very* well was how to take care of herself in a rough-house, all-in brawl. One of a large, mixed family, she learned to defend herself and working in saloons did nothing to make her forget her lessons.

Ducking her head, Pauline charged and butted Norah's body in a manner which would certainly have caused her immediate disqualification in a boxing ring. Norah gasped, went backwards, tripped and sat down. Then Pauline landed on top of her and bore her to the ground. In that moment Norah learned the vast difference between a sparring session wearing well-padded boxing gloves and the wild, anything-goes fury of a real fight.

Instinct came to Norah's rescue as Pauline sat astride her, grabbed two hands full of her hair. Twice the little blonde raised the head and slammed it on to the ground. A very effective tactic when used on the wooden floorboards of a saloon, the trick proved lacking on springy grass which cushioned the impact. While the blows hurt, they did not render Norah helpless. Arching her back, she gave a heave which rolled Pauline from her and brought her on top. Her fingers dug into the blonde's short, curly mop of hair and tore at it, but before she could make use of her extra weight Pauline reversed their positions once more.

For several seconds the girls rolled over and over in a wild tangle of flailing arms and thrashing legs. They tore at hair, drove knees into flesh, rained blows wildly and indiscriminately. All the time their teeth chopped at flesh and squeals of almost animal fury burst from them. Norah's blouse ripped away from her left shoulder under the blonde's clawing hands. Buttons popped from Pauline's shirt and its tail crawled out of the waistband of the levis.

Shrieking in rage and pain, Norah suddenly flung the lighter girl from her and came to her feet. Forcing down the animal rage, tinged with fear for she had the worst of the thrashing tangle due to Pauline's greater experience, Norah made herself think. As Pauline came up and charged into the attack, Norah once more adopted her boxing stance. Stabbing out a left jab of classic correctness, Norah caught Pauline in the face. Give her full due, Norah had learned well and landed two more jabs with the left so fast that she rocked the little blonde backwards and brought blood trickling from her nose. Pauline squealed and tried to rush in close, only to be stopped again by the stabbing fists. Pain tore through her and tears half-blinded her, warning her that she must come to grips and quickly or be battered unconscious.

When Pauline tried, Norah hooked a right into her belly and caused her to bend over. Up whipped the big girl's left under Pauline's offered chin and the blonde measured her length on the ground. If Norah had followed up immediately, she could have ended the fight. Shaken by the fury of Pauline's defence, Norah stood sucking in breaths of air and staring at the other girl. Then she advanced towards the sprawled-out shape.

"All right, you little whore!" Norah croaked. "Now we'll—"

In the brief time Pauline had recovered enough to see her danger. Waiting until Norah came close, she drove up her legs, slamming two bare feet into the other girl's midsection and hurling her backwards. Although winded, doubled over in agony and feeling ready to fetch up, Norah saw Pauline rise and knew why the blonde started to stagger towards the wagon. Ignoring the pain and nausea, forgetting boxing, Norah flung herself forward, locked her arms about Pauline's waist and brought the little girl to the ground.

Once again the wild, thrashing tangle worked up to fever pitch. Then they came to their feet, clinging to each other's hair with one hand, raining slaps and punches with the other, kicking at the other girl's shins. Pain and exhaustion filled both girls. They no longer screamed, their breath coming in saw-rasping gasps broken only when an extra hard blow or kick caused a hoarse squeal of protest. Blood ran from each woman's nose and their clothing had suffered. Pauline's shirt hung outside her pants and torn from buttonholes to hem. Norah no longer had a blouse on and her skirt had ripped from bottom to waistband, exposing her shapely legs in their tattered, kneeless stockings, one of which trailed around the top of her high-buttoned shoes.

There still did not appear to be any sight of one or the other girl gaining any ascendancy, Pauline's extra experience and desperation being offset by Norah having size and weight on her side.

Then Norah gave a surging shove which flung Pauline away from her. Pauline's back crashed into the wagon and she hung against it half dazed. Stumbling forward, Norah bent Pauline over the wagon and drove blow after blow into the blonde's face and upper body. Sick agony welled through Pauline, her fingers clawing at Norah's body. Then the blonde tried to reach her attacker's face, failed and her hand flopped back to touch one of the feed bowls. Desperately Pauline gripped the bowl and swung it round. The base of the bowl smashed into Norah's face, powered by an arm driven in desperation. Norah reeled backwards. Stumbling towards the tottering Norah, Pauline used the last of her waning strength to smash the bowl once more on to the other girl's head. Norah went down as if she had been pole-axed and the bowl fell from Pauline's hands as she sank to her knees.

Sick with exhaustion, half-naked and barely able to breathe, Pauline remained on her knees. From what seemed a long way off she heard voices. Raising her head, she managed to focus her swollen eyes, the left half-closed already, on the trio of men who came towards her.

"Yes sir," Elmhurt drawled. "Norah handled her real good."

"Sure was some whale of a fight," Laverick went on. "Reckon they'll come taw when they've rested?"

"Damn you!" yelled Loxton. "Help me with my sister."

"You fired us back there when we wouldn't let you come down and spoil the fun," Laverick reminded him. "So it looks like we got no call to take your orders."

"You—you don't know what to do with the girl," Loxton said, dropping to his knees by Norah.

"No," admitted Elmhurt, his eyes raking over Pauline's bare torso. "But I could maybe get me some good ideas."

Before Elmhurt could expand further on the matter, he heard the sound of hooves. A trio of riders; two white hard-cases and a filthy-looking Indian with a Winchester carbine gripped in his right hand, came down the slope. Dropping from their saddles, the trio walked towards Norah's party.

"Looks like you had some fuss here," Jack Sage remarked. "Must've been too busy watching them gals fighting to hear us coming up."

"So?" asked Elmhurt.

"We'll have that little blonde gal, feller," Sage said.

"Like he—!" Laverick began.

Joey Stinks held the carbine by the small of the butt, fingers through the loading lever and trigger-guard. Without troubling to put his left hand to the fore-grip, he raised the carbine and fired. Lead ripped into Laverick's body, spun him around and dropped him to the ground before he managed to get his gun clear. Even as Elmhurt grabbed for his revolver, Sage drew and sent a bullet into him. On his knees at his sister's side, Loxton could not have moved fast enough to save his life had he been a fighting man. Not that such a minor consideration appeared to bother the third hard-case. Drawing his gun, he started to line it on the scared face of the kneeling dude.

"Hold it!" roared a voice from on the rim.

Not only Norah's party had allowed themselves to become so interested that they failed to stay alert. With the end of the chase apparently in sight, Sage's group failed to notice a pair of men who had followed on their tracks.

One of the last arrivals was Flax Fannon. The other equalled Flax's height and looked even more powerfully built. Although expensive and cut in the fashion of a well-to-do rancher who still put in a full day's work with his crew, the second man's clothes were trail-dirty. Under a three-day stubble, his face was handsome, strong, commanding. Grey tinged his blond hair at the temples, yet he did not look old. Around his waist hung a good quality gunbelt, matched staghorn-handled Colt Artillery Model Peacemakers riding in fast-draw holsters. However, like Flax, the elder man put his faith at that time in a Winchester Centennial Model rifle.

"Waco!" spat Joey Stinks, recognizing the second of the newcomers, and started to raise the carbine.

No less keen-eyed, Waco identified the Indian and took no chances. He already held his rifle at the firing position and shot to kill. A flat-nosed .45 bullet driven by seventy-five grains of powder struck Joey Stinks between the eyes, burst out of the rear of his head and tumbled his lifeless body to the ground. Waco knew Joey Stinks' record too well to take chances and so shot to kill.

Swinging his revolver away from Loxton, the third hard-case fired a shot at the two Texans under the misguided belief that a handgun could equal a rifle over a range of some forty-five yards. Flax's Winchester cracked an answer and the man went down with a bullet in his chest.

Although badly wounded, Elmhurt managed to pull his gun and drive a bullet into Sage's back as the hard-case swung to meet the more pressing menace on the slope. Sage staggered forward, sent a bullet into the ground and then fell forward on to his face.

When Scobie Dale came charging on to the scene, his dun lathered and the pack speeding along around him, he found his fears for Pauline's safety justified but unnecessary. Waco had the situation well in hand. Already Flax tended to Pauline, Loxton looked to his sister and the U.S.

marshal knelt at Elmhurt's side, doing what he could for the man's wound.

"Pauline!" Scobie yelled, leaping from his horse and running to where the girl sat with her back resting against the wagon's rear off wheel.

"Sc—Scobie—" she gasped. "Oh, Scobie!"

"She's roughed up some," drawled Flax, bathing Pauline's face with a sopping wet bandana, "but you should see the other gal."

"Yeah!" Scobie growled, straightening up. "I reckon I should."

"Ease off there, Scobie!" Waco ordered. "Pauline did more than enough to her. Come and lend me a hand."

"How'd you get here just right, Waco?" asked Scobie as he helped the marshal with the bandaging of Elmhurt's wound.

"Flax and I met with Tex Rudbeck outside town," Waco explained. "Tex allowed to be taking a posse to look into Jervis Thorpe reporting that Kid Curry's bunch are hiding out at the Dooley place. Tex told me where you'd gone and when we saw Joey Stinks here leaving town we decided to trail him along."

"I'm not sorry you did," Scobie stated, then nodded to the Loxtons. "How do they figure in this?"

"I don't know yet, but figure to learn," Waco replied.

Half an hour later Loxton gave the two lawmen and Scobie the full story, his sister still being in no condition to talk. During her time in college Norah selected the fast-developing science of criminology as her choice for invading the field of male dominance, and made an extensive study. On graduating, she tried to gain entrance to some city's police department. At that time the only female officers were police matrons, mostly used for jailers in charge of women prisoners, and no department considered changing their policy. The refusal did not deter Norah, although it infuriated her. Being wealthy, she decided to form her own private detective agency and forced her weak-willed brother to join her.

After some success in the East, Norah decided they would try their hand on the more lucrative Western range country. With a few more successes behind her, Norah, along with all regular law enforcement departments and private agencies, became interested in the big Cattlemen's Trust Bank robbery. Shrewdly she connected the robbery to the news that Pauline must be found and killed. Hunting for Pauline, Norah believed that the little blonde could supply a clue to the robbery and might even know the men who pulled it. Norah knew that if she produced the lead which resulted in the capture of the recovery of the loot, she would receive much publicity and might even take away some of the trade which went to the Pinkerton and other rival agencies.

"I hope to God that this has knocked some sense into her," Loxton finished, dropping his voice so that his sister would not hear. "Whether it has or not, I'm quitting and going back East."

"You'd best take her with you," Waco grunted. "We've enough private law out here now without you setting up at it."

"Now we know," Scobie said, watching Loxton return to his sister. "What's next, Waco?"

"Well now," Waco replied. "That all depends on you— and the little blonde girl."

CHAPTER SIXTEEN

Pauline's Decision

"What's that?" Schuster barked, coming to his feet after hearing the news just brought by one of his men.

"It's the living truth, boss. Dale and the gal come into town. They're down at the livery barn right now."

Having the saloon to themselves, except for the bartender—who knew better than listen to private conversations when in that kind of company—Schuster did not trouble to hide his surprise at the man's information.

"But the Indian—" Thorpe began.

"Damn his stinking red hide!" Schuster growled. "If he lost the trail, I'll blow his stupid head off."

"He *must* have lost it," Thorpe said nervously. "Dale wouldn't have come here if he'd killed all three of them when they caught up to him."

"He might," Schuster answered. "Rudbeck's Dale's friend and Dale doesn't know we sent the marshal, along with every able-bodied man, out of town on a wild-goose chase."

"What do you aim to do, boss?" asked the man who brought the news.

"What we came out to do," replied Schuster.

"I'll wait here—" started Thorpe.

"The hell you will!" Schuster spat out. "You've lived

178

well and easy while I took all the risks for too long. It was your stupidity that started this and you'll be in it at the finish. Get Tonopah and the other boys here, Sam."

"Scared, Pauline gal?" asked Scobie, closing the door of the small cabin loaned to him as kennels for his pack when he first arrived in Desborough.

"N—No," she replied, having helped him by feeding the pack while he unhitched the wagon's team. "I always shiver at this time of day."

"I reckon you do," Scobie smiled and gave her a gentle hug which brought a gasp of pain. "Sorry, gal."

"That's all right," she answered. "I'm only bruises where there're no bumps or lumps."

"You should pick a fight with somebody your own size," drawled Scobie. "I reckon it's time we started."

Taking up his Lightning rifle, Scobie started to walk from the cabin with Pauline at his side. He held the rifle in both hands, negligently before him but ready for use. Before they had taken many steps, he and the girl saw Schuster, Thorpe and Kid Tonopah approaching along the alley between the livery barn and the next building.

Once clear of the building, the three men halted so as to block Scobie and Pauline's path. Schuster had to look twice before he recognized the girl, being used to seeing her with longer hair and in a dress. Instead she wore the new shirt and levis, while her face showed marks of the fight with Norah. Not that Schuster worried how she came by her battle-scars. His eyes went to where Strike stood eating alongside the wagon. With something like relief, Schuster saw no sign of the rest of the pack. He had not fancied tangling with Scobie's full pack of fighting hounds.

"You're in bad company, Dale," Schuster said. "That girl with you came to ask Mr. Thorpe for help and robbed him."

"She did, huh?" Scobie drawled. "That's not what she told me."

"I don't expect it is," Schuster answered, hearing Tonopah move restlessly at his side and hoping the young man had taken to heart threats made as to his fate should he provoke trouble.

"Reckon I'd better take her to the marshal's office," Scobie said.

"You don't need to bother. We'll tend to her."

"You said she robbed Mr. Thorpe," Scobie remarked. "That's not what one of those fellers with the Indian told me."

"Sage didn't know I killed the teller!" Thorpe screeched.

"You damned fool, Thorpe!" Schuster roared and reached for his gun.

At the same instant Kid Tonopah became aware of something menacingly significant in the way Scobie held his rifle. Although it hung in a casual manner, Scobie gripped it by the small of the butt and his forefinger was inside the trigger-guard. An experienced man like Scobie Dale did not place his finger on the trigger unless expecting to use the rifle real soon.

Even as the thought came into Tonopah's head and sent his hand driving for the butt of the holstered Colt, he saw Scobie go into action.

From being held casually relaxed, Scobie brought the rifle around and hip-high to point at Schuster. There would be little or no time to spare if Scobie wanted to stay alive. Fortunately, the three men stood bunched together instead of fanning out into a better fighting formation.

Flame lashed from the Lightning's barrel and a .50 calibre, solid lead bullet tore into Schuster's belly with a force that flung the man backwards, made him drop his gun, knocking all the fight out of him. So far Scobie had guessed correctly, figuring Schuster to be the fastest of the trio. Everything now depended on one of the Lightning rifle's advantages. Controlling as well as possible the recoil caused by ninety-five grains of powder exploding inside it, Scobie began to swing the rifle in the direction of Kid Tonopah. Holding back the trigger in its firing position, Scobie used a reciprocating action of his left hand to flick back the slide, eject the empty case, replace it with a loaded bullet, fire the round and repeat the cycle.

No other manually operated rifle, not even the traditional and fabled lever action Winchester, could equal the Lightning's speed of fire when handled in such a manner. A second bullet tore through the swinging flap of Schuster's jacket, a third passed between him and Tonopah, then the fourth ripped into the amazed young gun-hand as he froze into shocked immobility at the volume of fire. Spinning around with the back of his head burst open from the bullet's exit—the rifle's recoil forced Scobie to shoot higher each time—Tonopah dropped his gun and fell on to Schuster's body.

Everything seemed to be happening at once. Turning, Thorpe tried to run as the remainder of Schuster's hired hands burst into view from different points. It was a gun-trap, but not quite in the way Schuster planned.

"Strike!" Pauline yelled. "Get him!"

Having raised his head at the first shot, Strike hurled forward to the defence of his master. Racing by Scobie and the girl, the big rottweiler overtook Thorpe, hurled himself into the air and closed his powerful, crashing jaws on the man's arm. Struck by Strike's chunky, heavy body, Thorpe crashed to the ground and screamed for help.

Flicking another bullet into the rifle's chamber, Scobie started to swing around and meet the new menace. While he would have preferred to use his dogs for added protection, that had been impossible without endangering the lives of Waco and Flax Fannon. On hearing the shooting, they put in their appearance from their place of concealment inside the wagon, having left the wounded men in Loxton's care outside town.

Waco came into view at the front of the wagon and threw a shot with his right-hand Colt, tumbling over one of a pair of men who dashed around the other end of the livery barn. Before Scobie or Waco could make a move against the second man, he screeched, a shot sounded from Main Street and he went down with a bullet in his shoulder.

Bounding out of the rear of the wagon, Flax Fannon tossed a couple of shots in the direction of two more Schuster men, but without effect. They did not return his fire, seeing their employer sprawled on the ground. Being of the kind who fought only for pay, neither relished a gun-battle which offered no wages at its end. Turning, they ran back to Main Street, collected the waiting horses and, shortly followed by the last of their party, left Desborough at full gallop.

Scobie handed his rifle to the girl, then darted forward to drag Strike away from Thorpe. Sobbing, babbling, the politician glared with terrified eyes from the rottweiler to the advancing men. Marshal Tex Rudbeck strolled along the side alley from Main Street and kicked the revolver away from the man his shot wounded.

"I'd sure as hell like to know why the peace's been disturbed in my town," he told Waco indignantly.

"How'd you get back here so quick?" Waco smiled, glancing around to make sure everything was under control.

"It didn't set right with me that Thorpe'd help a peace officer against an owl-hoot," Rudbeck explained. "So I left the posse out there and come in careful like."

"I'm sorry I played them close to the vest, Tex," apologized Waco. "No offence meant. But I didn't want to tip my hand in case any of your posse worked for Schuster."

"None took—as long as I get to know what's happened."

"I reckon Mr. Thorpe can tell us most of that," drawled Waco, looking to where Pauline profanely quietened the dogs in the cabin. "Him and the gal between them."

Thorpe talked, giving enough information to ensure the success of Waco's clean-up in Wyoming and the adjacent States. Although the politician tried to lay all the blame for the Planner's activities on to Schuster, the other man lived long enough to thoroughly implicate the politician. Learning of his partner's attempt, Schuster gave full details of the Cattleman's Trust Bank business, including the fact that all the negotiable bonds and most of the money could be found in the safe in Thorpe's office. That knowledge, plus a signed death-bed confession, gave Waco all he needed to convict Thorpe.

Carrying her travelling bag, although still dressed in shirt and levis, Pauline stood before Desborough's Wells Fargo office on the day after the fight. While she would still be required to give evidence at Thorpe's trial, Waco decided she could be let go her own way until needed. Everybody involved in the Planner's affairs would be too busy hiding their tracks, or fleeing the country, to worry about Thorpe, and the girl's evidence would hardly be needed to convict him so she was unlikely to be bothered again.

If Schuster had told the truth, Pauline and Scobie stood to share the reward offered by the Cattlemen's Trust Bank. With her portion, the girl could go East, buy the right kind of clothes and jewellery, then find work in a good-class saloon which offered better opportunities than any in the West.

Her eyes went to where Scobie climbed on to his

wagon. Word had come in that a cougar killed forty sheep during a night's blood-lust at Newcastle and Scobie was on his way to hunt it down. If Pauline wished, she could go with him, as his wife.

Only she did not want to go. A girl would be a fool and worse to tangle with a foot-loose hound dog man whose only home was a Rocker ambulance—not that it made a bad home though. Pauline chopped off her thoughts on the matter and tried to direct them to cold winters, a hungry belly, rags to wear—

Whip walked across the street, wagging his tail and rubbing against her leg as if trying to tell her they were ready to move. Gently she rubbed the dog's ears and looked at the rest of the pack.

No, damn it, a girl would be a fool to give up working in a saloon with—drunks pawing her, breathing whisky-fumes into her face, stamping on her feet when dancing. She could wear fine clothes—but would not feel the warm touch of grass between her toes. Desperately Pauline tried to make herself think of all the good times spent in saloons and could only bring up a picture of Scobie. She remembered his gentleness, the way Vixen licked her hand as she fought to save the life of a weak pup, how the pack grew to accept her. A girl would be a fool—

"So I'm a fool," she said and dropped the bag which contained all her saloon clothing. "Let's go, Whip."

With that Pauline walked across the street and climbed onto the wagon alongside her hound dog man.